One Christmas With You

Copyright © 2024 by Mari Suggs.

All rights reserved. No part of this book may be used or reproduced in any form whatsoever without written permission except in the case of brief quotations in critical articles or reviews.

This book is a work of fiction. Names, characters, businesses, organizations, places, events and incidents either are the product of the author's imagination or are used fictitiously. Any resemblance to actual persons, living or dead, events, or locales is entirely coincidental.

Printed in the United States of America.

For more information, or to book an event, contact:
mari@marisuggs.com
http://www.marisuggs.com

ISBN - Paperback: 979-8-8693-0171-0
First Edition: November 2024

For Mami, because you loved that I became a writer.

Mari Suggs

CHAPTER 1

Eloise

The last time I took time off from work, things happened that still bring heat to my cheeks and confusion to my heart. They are secrets known only to me.

It's December 21st, and as I look around West Memorial Regional Hospital, I feel disappointed by the lack of Christmas spirit. The staff had only added some garland to their desks, with no sign of festive treats in sight. If I had the time, I would have loved to bring in homemade goodies, a tree, and some ornaments to brighten up the place. But with the gruelling schedule I've been keeping, I simply don't have the time. Even sleep is a luxury I can barely afford.

A small exhale escapes my lips. I'm exhausted. After what seems like an interminable year, if not four, I'm only one chart away from beginning my much-needed vacation.

Whenever people ask me what it's like being an ER doctor, I give them the answer they want to hear: rewarding. I've repeated it so many times it sounds like the truth, but the reality is far from it. The job is mostly stressful and depressing as I can't seem to leave the work at work. It's been affecting my mental health and sleep.

I know I'm good at what I do, but I also know that it's not a good fit for me. I've known it for a while now, but with only one year left in my residency, it seems pointless if not irresponsible to switch careers now, as if I could anyway.

As I finish up the chart for my last patient of the day, I breathe a sigh of relief. Thankfully, she's going to be okay. She thought she was having a heart attack, but it turned out to be just indigestion. Now, she's on her way back home to finish planning her big family Christmas gathering. It was heartwarming to see how this minor incident had changed her perspective on what had previously been a very stressful season. It's these happy endings that have kept me going over the last few years. But I wonder if they'll be enough to sustain me for the rest of my career.

I do some quick mental calculations. I'm only twenty-nine, and if I retire at sixty-two, I still have thirty-three more years to go. And so the countdown begins.

Pushing aside thoughts of the next thirty-three years of my life, I try to focus on something more pleasant, like my upcoming vacation. I have a few days off to celebrate Christmas with just my mom and dad. It isn't the ideal Christmas, not like the ones you see on the Hallmark channel. I always wanted that kind of Christmas, to be surrounded by a joyful and warm family, one that loves baked goods and a mom who brings me hot cocoa with marshmallows for no reason at all. But that's just not the family I was born into.

Christmas with my family is more like a stuffy dinner party where everyone is still talking about work. Unfortunately, this means more hospital talk since my dad is a surgeon. My mom is not a doctor but is the perfect doctor's wife and hostess. The number of parties and benefits she organizes in one year is exhausting to hear about. I manage to avoid all of it by working. It's the only excuse they'll accept. The only bummer is that I am actually working.

In the last four years, I've only taken one

weekend off and I wish I could forget it ever happened—for many reasons. I'm not in the habit of taking time off, in fact, I always work through holidays. But this year, my parents asked, no, demanded, that I take Christmas off. I didn't have a ready excuse and so I said I would.

Truthfully, when I requested the time off, I didn't think it would be approved. Holidays are usually the busiest times for the ER. But to my surprise my boss insisted I not only take Christmas off, but also an additional three days. I argued there was no need, but he wouldn't hear of it. I knew deep down that I desperately needed the break. After working doubles nearly every day for the past six months, I am completely burned out.

As my shift comes to an end and my charts are updated, my vacation is finally here. But first, I'm heading to the cafeteria to meet my best friend, Susie.

The moment I spot her, my mood instantly shifts from drained to alive. There's just something about her energy that's infectious and makes me forget about all my worries.

Maybe it's the way she always greets me with a smile, or the way she can make even the most mundane tasks seem fun and exciting. Whatever it is, I'm grateful for it.

"Eloise, over here," she yells across the room.

She's impossible to miss. She's waving at me like

she's hitchhiking for a ride. I laugh because this is so typical of her. She's the most over-the-top person I know and the most authentic. She's unapologetically unabashed and I love her for it.

We became instant friends the day I arrived at West Memorial Regional, and now she's one of the most important people in my life. I don't know how I would've made it through some of the most difficult days here without her. What will I do now that she's leaving? The Human Resources department is going to fall apart, I just know it. But I understand her desire to be home with her baby. I would do the same.

Susie is thirty-five, married to Dave, and expecting her first baby girl any day now, and she's positively thriving in this magical stage of life.

Despite the physical and emotional demands of pregnancy, Susie is glowing. Her skin is radiant, and her dark wavy hair is fuller and shinier than ever before. She's a true vision of beauty.

While I've heard other expectant mothers complain about the discomfort and challenges that come with pregnancy, Susie seems to take everything in stride. She's determined to enjoy every moment of this precious time, savouring the joys and wonders that come with bringing a new life into the world.

As I walk the busy hospital cafeteria, my attention is focused solely on my dear friend, who I'm eager to see. I bypass the food and head straight toward her.

And then, as I draw closer, I hear it; the familiar sound of Christmas, "It's the Most Wonderful Time of the Year," is playing over the cafeteria speakers. My fading laughter turns into a broad smile, and I feel a rush of holiday spirit fill me up. This is my favorite Christmas song, and every time I hear it, I'm reminded of all the warmth, good cheer, and love that this time of year represents.

"Hi there," I say as I plop down onto the chair, feeling the exhaustion setting in.

"Are you serious?" she exclaims, looking at me with disbelief.

I look down at my clothes and smooth out my hair expecting to find something unpleasant.

"What is it?" I ask, concerned.

"How do you manage to look so put together even after a long shift?" She's rummaging through her purse, searching for something.

"Susie! You scared me, I thought I was walking around with one of my patients' blood all over me."

She chuckles and quickly retrieves a mirror and lip gloss from her purse. "I mean, you've been working since 2 a.m., right?" she asks, applying a bit of lip gloss. She pulls the mirror back, turning it as if she can't see herself properly.

"Something like that," I reply, nodding in agreement.

I stare at her quizzically as she holds the mirror at arm's length. "What are you doing?" I ask, curious as to why she is examining herself from such a distance.

"Ugh, no good angle," she groans, throwing the mirror and lip gloss back into her purse. "How can you possibly still look this gorgeous with no sleep? Your hair is intact, and there are no bags under your eyes. It must be a doctor thing," she corrects herself, shaking a finger before I even have a chance to respond. "Or maybe it's a 20's thing. Or maybe it's just a you thing," she adds.

She's talking but it doesn't seem like she's even talking to me.

"Thank you. But stop it. You're crazy."

I feel a twinge of self-consciousness as she compliments my appearance. My hair is pulled back in a messy bun, and my work clothes hardly make for a glamorous look. But at the same time, I appreciate her kind words and the way they make me feel seen.

"So, I'm officially a free woman," I say, tapping the table and leaning back in my chair.

Despite my initial reluctance to take four consecutive days off, I find myself feeling surprisingly relieved as I think more about the upcoming break.

"Finally, it only took you four years to get a day off," she says.

"You're forgetting about six months ago," I remind her, but I don't know why. There is nothing in the world I want more than to forget about that weekend.

"Oh yeah, the one where you came back sadder than when you left?"

I don't say anything in response. A part of me is afraid that if I open my mouth, she will see right through me.

Things happened that weekend I've kept hidden from Susie, things I'm ashamed of and afraid to share. What would she say? What would she think if she knew?

"How does it feel?" I ask her, changing the subject to avoid any further discussion about that fateful weekend.

"That it's my last day?"

"Yeah," I say with intrigue, like a child asking for candy. Susie is the only one who knows how much I really don't want to be a doctor.

"Frigging amazing."

"Wow, you're so lucky."

"Eloise," she says grabbing my hand. "I'm not lucky. I just know what I want and I'm not afraid to go for it. I wanted a baby, so, I got pregnant. I wanted to raise my baby, so, I quit my job. I'm not afraid of making decisions because my parent's will get mad at me."

Ouch.

Susie sits back in her chair, seemingly finished with our conversation. But then she speaks again, her voice gentle and caring.

"This," she says, gesturing to the bustling hospital cafeteria around us, "isn't for you. Explain it to your parents. They'll understand."

"It's not that simple," I say, slouching in my chair like a child.

She looks at me with a deep sense of empathy in her eyes. "It is," she says softly, her voice filled with a mixture of sadness and understanding.

It's difficult to explain the complexity of my feelings. On one hand, I am a grown woman with a successful career and a sense of independence. Yet, when it comes to my parents, I feel like a child again, afraid of letting them down and not meeting their expectations. The thought of confronting them fills me with dread and anxiety, and I can't help but wonder what they would think of me if they knew the whole truth. It's a delicate balance between pleasing them and finding my own happiness, and sometimes it feels like I'll never be able to strike that balance.

As Susie looks at me with pity, I imagine how she would react if she knew what happened six months ago. If she thinks not standing up to my parents is cowardly, she would surely be livid over this.

CHAPTER 2

Eloise

Six months ago, I requested a weekend off to surprise my boyfriend of two years, Dr. Chris Sullivan, who was attending a medical conference in Hawaii. Our relationship had been rocky, and I was feeling guilty. I needed things to work between us, but it seemed like our relationship was slipping away. I knew I needed to put in more effort if things were ever going to work out between us. Then maybe, just maybe, I could learn to love him someday.

He had been at the conference for an entire week and I thought it would be a great idea to surprise him with my unexpected visit. However, my surprise didn't turn out the way I had hoped.

After a gruelling flight, my mind was foggy and

my body ached. All I could think about was collapsing into bed and letting sleep take me away—not exactly the romantic vacation I initially aimed for. But as I stumbled through the lobby of the hotel, I saw something that made me question whether I was even awake.

There he was, Chris, my boyfriend of two years, locked in an embrace with another woman. I froze, unable to comprehend what I was seeing. Was this some kind of twisted dream? Or had my eyes finally given up on me after months of non-stop work? But as I blinked and shook my head, the truth smacked me awake. This wasn't a dream.

So, there I was, playing my own version of hide-and-seek. I hid behind a waiter, and when he moved, I quickly scurried behind another one. When I was finally close enough, my heart sank. He was actually cheating on me.

I'd like to say that I walked right up to him and gave him a piece of my mind, but I didn't. Without him even knowing I was there, I turned right back around and jumped on another plane back home. This is one of many things that happened that weekend that I haven't shared with anyone, not even Susie.

I shook away the memory, and the reality that I'm still with Chris.

"The Most Wonderful Time of the Year" is now

playing louder because it's not just coming from the speakers above, but from my ringtone. Changing my ringtone was the only festive thing I managed to do for Christmas since it required very little effort.

Still slouching in my chair, I pull the phone from my pocket and see that it's my dad. I pop up like a jack-in-the-box and straighten as if he could see me.

Susie shoots me a, what the heck look.

"Hi Dad," I say into the phone, staring at her.

She follows the look with an "oh," understanding my sudden shift.

"Eloise are you with Chris?" he asks.

"No, why?"

"As you know, the Sullivans are joining us for Christmas, and there's a matter I need to attend with Chris before then. But I haven't been able to reach him."

"What, why?" I practically yell into the phone.

"Pardon me?" my dad replies, confused by my sudden outburst.

"I mean, doesn't Chris have to work on Christmas?" I say, trying to soften my tone this time.

"Eloise, obviously not," he says, his voice tinged with frustration.

"Right."

"Well, when you see him, have him call me." He hangs up and the moment he does, I see Chris coming toward me.

Chris is older than me by ten years. He's not the most physically attractive man. His dark hair is slightly receding, his height is average, and he rarely ever visits a gym. But I could've overlooked all those things. It's his pompous attitude that I can't stomach.

"Peaches," he says kissing me on the top of the head. "Susan." He doesn't look at Susie when he greets her but at least he acknowledged her this time.

"It's Susie, Christopher."

"Dr. Sullivan," he counters.

"Ugh," she says loud enough for him to hear.

She stands and leaves to throw her plate away. Susie's not a fan of Chris and can't stand being around him. It's rare when my two worlds collide. I do a nice job of keeping them separate, even though we work in the same place.

My parents worked very hard to get me to date Chris. Yet, I can't blame them because I was the one who said yes when he asked me out. I wanted my parents to get off my back. Once I said yes, I kept saying yes to avoid saying no. I know it's silly, but my M.O. is to avoid confrontation at all costs. Even if it's at my own expense.

The Sullivans have been friends with my parents forever, but I hardly saw Chris because he was away at boarding school or his prestigious university, or medical school.

"Did you hear the good news? Our families are

celebrating Christmas together," he says, typing out a message on his phone. "Afterward, I have a hotel booked for us. I thought a change of scenery would do us some good." He arches an eyebrow in my direction. "It's going to be great."

I know exactly what he's talking about. We haven't exactly been a couple lately, more like roommates.

"Um—I... I..." I stutter as I search for an answer to this problem.

"What is it," he says impatiently urging me to speak, still not looking up from his phone.

By now Susie's back. I look at her hoping she goes along. I know she will. She's very insightful so I don't think about it too long, I just go for it.

"I actually won't be there. I have to work. I was asked to fill in at East Memorial."

"Nonsense. I'll speak to them."

"No!" I say, a bit too quickly. "You know how it'll look if you or my dad interfere on my behalf. It will undermine me. Please don't," I say looking between him and Susie.

After a moment, he says, "Fine then. But it won't be the same without you," finally looking at me.

"I'm sorry," I say, not really meaning it.

He kisses me again on top of my head and walks away without saying goodbye to Susie.

I'm relieved that I won't have to spend Christmas

with him. Though I haven't broken up with him, I might as well have. We haven't had sex in six months or been on anything that resembles a date. I have all the hours at work to thank for that. *I can't believe I just got away with that.*

"What now?" asks Susie.

But before I'm able to explain, my phone is ringing again. It's Mom and I answer quickly.

"Hello."

"Eloise, what is this nonsense about you working? We agreed that you would take Christmas off."

Wow! News travels fast in this group.

"Mom, I did. It was a last-minute thing. I can't get out of it."

"Your father will call and talk to your boss."

There's just no way that's happening.

"No!" A similar shriek to the one earlier escapes my mouth but I self-correct, quickly. "Mom, you know I don't want you guys interfering in my work. Please! There's always next year," I plead hoping she just lets it go.

There's a brief silence, and I pray that she's considering the consequences of their interference.

"Very well, Eloise. At least call and wish us a Merry Christmas."

"I will."

We hang up and Susie is looking at me very confused.

"They're throwing a big party with their country club friends and it's probably going to be a benefit of some sort. I can't do it."

I lie because I don't want her to know that I'm trying to avoid Chris. I would have to explain why. I'm not ready to do that yet.

The truth is I'm afraid to go now that he's going to be there because I can't avoid him much longer and his patience is wearing thin. It's time for me to either break up with him or forget what happened. If I stay with him and tell Susie, she is going to lose all respect for me. If I break up with him, I'll have to explain it to my parents. No. Not yet. I'm not ready to let anyone know what happened.

"Okay, so what are you going to do for Christmas?" she asks.

I let out a small breath because she bought my lie. *I'm a terrible friend.* The lies just keep piling up.

"Nothing."

"You are not staying home alone," she says, rubbing her baby pump.

"Well, going to my parent's house is not an option."

"Then it's settled. You're coming with us."

"What? No. I can't impose on your family at Christmas."

"You're not. You know my parents live in Maple Hallow. I don't know how you've managed to avoid going to the most magical Christmas town in the entire country, but that's about to change," she tells me, adamantly. "We leave tomorrow."

"I don't know," I say, but I'm really contemplating it.

It could be fun. And if her family is anything like she is, I might just get my Hallmark Christmas after all.

She grabs my hand and says, "Eloise, you're my best friend. I would love it if you met my family. They're the most welcoming bunch you'll ever meet. They'll be so happy to have you.

"Are you sure?" I ask.

"Of course, I am. It'll be fun."

"Okay then. Yes, I'll come, thank you," I finally say.

CHAPTER 3

Trevor

Looking around my apartment, I feel empowered by the sight of it. The last of my things are finally gone, leaving nothing but the clothes on my back, the ones in my backpack, and my camera. I am finally free.

Embracing minimalism has allowed me to prioritize what truly matters in my life. I've learned to let go of the unnecessary clutter and distractions that once held me back. As a result, I feel more in control and focused on what really brings me joy and fulfillment. It's not always easy, but I know that this path is right for me and I'm eager to see where it leads me.

I'm excited to wrap up the last bit of business before flying home for the holidays. I'll be driving my motorcycle to the gym I used to own and meeting Kyle, who not only bought my gym but my bike too.

Is it too early to call myself a nomad? I don't think so. As much as I'd love to be jetting off to Europe right now to start my new life as a traveler, I'm heading to my hometown, which is known for its extreme holiday festivities. I know how important the holidays are to my family, especially my mom, and she would be devastated if I didn't make it back.

My childhood home is a cabin in Georgia, nestled in the town of Maple Hallow. It is a picturesque town where time seems to slow down. The streets are lined with quaint shops, each with its own unique charm. The air is crisp and fresh, carrying the scent of pine and wood-burning stoves.

But what really sets Maple Hollow apart is its obsession with holiday celebrations. It seems that every holiday is an opportunity for the town to go all out, but nothing compares to the extravagance of Christmas. The entire town transforms into a winter wonderland, with twinkling lights adorning every tree and building.

The locals are warm and welcoming, eager to share their holiday cheer with anyone who comes to visit. Maple Hollow may be a small town, but during the Christmas season, it's a place of magic and wonder that leaves a lasting impression on all who experience it.

Okay, I'll confess that as a child, I enjoyed it. And, when I was a teenager, I volunteered frequently during the peak season to fulfill my community service hours. However, as a 30-year-old man, I've lost interest in it, and as a minimalist, the town's excesses are sometimes overwhelming.

It's snowing today, so driving the motorcycle to the gym was probably not the best idea, but I had no choice. Today is my last day in Colorado and I had to drop off the bike before heading out. As I pull into the parking lot, I'm eager to get inside, but before I do I grab my camera to take a picture. Photography has become a newfound passion of mine, and I've challenged myself to capture just one photo per memorable moment. One photo is all it takes to make a lasting impression.

When I first started getting into photography, I wondered if I could apply my minimalism to it as well. No sense in taking a hundred photos of the same thing when I only need one. I take my one shot then head inside away from the snow.

Even though I've sold it, I still love this gym. It's not your run-of-the-mill fitness center, it's a ninja gym. People who come here come to train so they can qualify for the TV show Ninja Warrior. I used to train a lot of my clients myself, but recently I hired one of the show's winners to take over. I knew he would be better qualified for the job, and I was right. Five guys he's trained at my gym have made it onto the show and almost won. This success means that the gym has the potential to expand to other locations. I've received numerous requests to open branches in other states, but I'm not interested at the moment. Maybe someday, but for now, I'm focused on traveling.

Kyle sits behind the counter, intently staring at his laptop, likely at a spreadsheet. He's always been the numbers guy, and while he may not have any experience in training, he knows how to keep a good system in place. Hiring the best trainers to work with the guys who come to the gym to prepare for Ninja Warrior has proven to be a successful formula. With the growing popularity of the show and the gym, he won't have any trouble finding talented trainers to continue the work. I'm glad he'll be running things now; I'm not sure I would have felt as comfortable letting it go to anyone else.

When Kyle came to me three years ago, he was your typical burned-out, overweight, forty-something guy. He walked into my gym after quitting his job in finance, claiming the long hours and stress had nearly killed him. I could relate to his situation as I had my own experience in finance right out of college. But unlike Kyle, I didn't spend twenty years thinking about my exit. I only gave it two years before pursuing my passion for fitness.

Kyle expressed to me that he was looking for a job that could provide financial stability for his family, while also helping him improve his physical health. The weight of his numerous responsibilities was evident on his tired face. I hired him on the spot to run the office.

His transformation from where he started to the confident and fit owner of a successful gym is truly remarkable. Now, seeing him behind the counter, looking healthier and happier than ever, makes me proud to have played a part in his journey.

He looks up when he hears me come in.

"Hey Trevor," he says.

"Hey, how's it going?" As predicted, a spreadsheet is on the screen.

"Budgets, you know how it is."

"I do, my friend."

"You're all packed?" he asks.

"All packed and ready to go," I reply, pointing to my backpack. "Here you go," I add, extending the bike keys toward him.

"Thanks!"

"You got it."

"I don't know how you do that," he mused.

"What, pack?"

"No, live in lack," he clarifies.

"I don't live in lack," I laugh, shaking my head in amusement.

"Don't you ever want things?"

"No, I don't. I want experiences. Which is exactly what I'm going to get once the holidays are over."

"Of course you do. I bet you're looking forward to flying again?" he says, teasing.

"What do you mean?" I ask, a bit confused.

"Well, last time you flew you scored, no?"

"Wow, that again? I shouldn't have told you."

"C'mon lighten up. You met a cute girl on a flight, and you hooked up. That's how it's done."

"I don't know how many times I have to tell you. It wasn't like that."

"Yeah, I know she was "special," he says, mocking me.

I'm about to protest but he's already backing away from me.

"I have to grab something from the back. Can you stay here for a few minutes?" he asks.

"Perfect timing," I tell him.

"Lucky me," he laughs turning into the storage room.

Sitting behind the counter, I feel a nagging sense of discomfort at Kyle's comments. It seems as though he doesn't fully grasp what happened, or perhaps he simply doesn't understand how deeply it affected me. And as I think about it more, I realize that maybe it's my fault.

Perhaps I never fully explained what happened or how I truly felt about her, leaving room for misunderstandings and misconceptions.

Regret washes over me. I should've known better than to tell anyone about that day. I pride myself on being a man of discretion, someone who can keep a secret and never kiss and tell. But in a moment of weakness, I let my guard down and shared more than I should've.

Six months ago, while I was flying back home from a friend's wedding in Hawaii, fate intervened and seated me next to a charming woman. Little did I know, we were about to spend the next twenty-four hours together after our connecting flight was delayed and eventually cancelled.

She was traveling to Georgia from Hawaii, while I was heading back home to Colorado. Despite sharing intimate moments, we didn't have time to really get to know each other. I tried asking her questions to learn more about her, but every time I did, she was vague with personal details. I don't even know her last name, which only added to the mystery and intrigue surrounding our brief encounter.

Initially, I struck up a conversation with her just to be friendly as she seemed upset. I never anticipated how events would unfold between us. I've told Kyle this, but he likes to tease me all the same.

Perhaps Kyle refuses to believe me because no matter how many times I tell him it was just a chance encounter my tone says otherwise. The truth is, I can't deny that I still think about her, especially during this season which she adored so much.

She painted a picture of the holidays that was nothing short of magical, straight out of a movie where everything is perfect, and it even snows on Christmas morning. For a brief moment, she made me forget that it was during Christmas one year when I almost lost my life.

I'm lost in my thoughts, and the sudden ringing of my phone snaps me back to reality. It's my sister, Susie.

"Hey, sis," I answer, pushing away the memory of that day.

"Hey! When's your flight?"

"I have to be at the airport in an hour."

"Well, not sure if you've seen, but there's a big snowstorm expected tonight. Will you be in before then?"

"Yeah, for sure."

"Great. Also, I should let you know that my best friend is joining us," she says.

"Sounds like fun, the more the merrier," I reply.

"I knew you wouldn't mind. I just wanted to give you a heads-up so you can make an extra effort to make her feel welcome. She's feeling like she's imposing," she explains.

"Consider it done," I assure her.

"Actually, there's one more thing. Can I ask you for a favor?" she adds. I know my sister's requests usually involve something I would never consider doing myself.

"Sure," I respond cautiously.

"You're at the gym, right?"

"I am."

She doesn't know that I've sold it, only my mom knows. I've asked her not to say anything as I want to break the news to my dad in person. I'm dreading that conversation since he's likely to respond with his typical disapproval. I plan to wait until the last day we're all together to avoid putting a damper on the holiday festivities.

"Great!" Her excitement is palpable over the phone. "Could you do me a favor and swing by the Christmas shop next door and pick up an ornament for me?"

"Sus, you know I hate going into those stores. Why can't you do it?"

"Because I'm already on my way to pick her up, and the idea just came to me. Pretty please?" she pleads.

Reluctantly, I agree to her request. After all, it's for my sister, whom I love, and it's not a big deal since I won't be keeping it.

"Okay, what kind of ornament are you thinking of?" I ask.

"Something nice, and I want her name engraved on it."

"No problem. What's her name?" I grab a pen and paper to write it down.

"Eloise."

"Eloise?" I repeat, slightly taken aback.

"Yeah, her parents are old-fashioned."

"Interesting. I once met an Eloise."

"I'm sure you did."

"What's that supposed to mean?"

"It means you're a girl magnet. Speaking of which, no funny business with Eloise," she warns.

"What? Me? Never!" I say, feigning innocence.

Growing up, I've been known to have a crush or two on her friends. It was quite funny, getting a rise out of her. That is until it turned on me. It wasn't as funny when she started getting interested in my friends.

"Don't give me that. You know our rule: no messing around with each other's friends," she reminds me. "Just try to make her feel at home like a brother would."

"Relax, Sus. I'm not looking to date."

"That doesn't matter. Women always flock to you."

"I can't help it if I'm irresistible," I tease, trying to

get a rise out of my big sister.

"Please, you wish. Seriously, Eloise is the whole package, just your type. Gorgeous, funny, kind, and wonderful. But she's my best friend and I don't want you complicating things by flirting with her."

"Okay, okay, you got it."

"Now you better hurry. I don't want you missing your flight and ruining Christmas for everyone."

"Don't worry, I'm out the door."

"Okay, love you."

"Love you too," I say before ending the call.

After hanging up, I'm perplexed. Eloise isn't exactly a name you hear every day. If I remember correctly, "my Eloise" was heading to Georgia. But she can't be the same person as my sister's friend, can she? I immediately dismiss the thought as unlikely.

When Kyle returns, I say my goodbyes, realizing that it might be the last time we see each other. Wanting to ensure that he knows I'm available to help if needed, I reiterate that I am just a phone call away. After our farewell, I make my way to the airport, but not before picking up that ornament for Susie.

CHAPTER 4

Eloise

It's 9 a.m. and I'm still in bed on a Wednesday morning. I can't remember the last time I did this. In fact, it feels like I've never done this. I was raised to always be on the go, even as a little girl. Even during summers. Summer! The resentment bubbles up.

Summer is that time of year when kids should be free to lounge by a pool and bask in the glory of sleeping in. Not me, though. Every summer, I had the privilege of being shuttled around from one activity to another, with barely a moment to catch my breath. Piano lessons, tennis lessons, and even the dreaded etiquette school. Thankfully, etiquette school was only for one summer—thanks to the fact that I was a quick study. I knew I had to keep up the charade of being the perfect young lady, lest I be forced to return to that place of agony again. So I kept up the facade of being the polite, well-behaved little girl my mom had always wanted me to be. The only thing is, it stuck. I'm nothing if not polite.

Despite the bitterness that threatens to consume me, I remind myself that it's the most wonderful time of the year, it's Christmas and this is no time for negativity, sadness, or ugliness. And so, I make a conscious decision to change my mood and I know just what will do it.

"Hey Google!" I shout, my voice echoing through the room. "Play traditional Christmas music!" The ever-obliging Google Home chirps back, "Playing traditional Christmas music," and before I know it, my room is filled with the merry tunes of the season. I can feel the joy bubbling up inside me as I listen, and I know that this is going to be one heck of a Christmas break.

Grogginess is clinging to me like a persistent little cloud. But I refuse to let it get the best of me. With a determined spirit, I start to stretch and twist my body, feeling the satisfying little pops and cracks as I loosen up my muscles. Ah, yes - that's the stuff.

As I glance around my room, I'm disappointed. Where is the Christmas tree? The festive lights? The stockings on the fireplace? It's like my house doesn't even know that Christmas is here!

Other than switching the ringtone, the only Christmas-related task I've tackled so far is browsing online for gifts for my parents. Unfortunately, nothing felt quite perfect. Probably because I really enjoy doing my shopping in person, and lately it's been tough to find the time.

Despite my efforts to remain optimistic, I question whether or not things will ever change. Especially when I see how incredibly busy my dad is as a top surgeon at the hospital.

I groan and pull my plush red blanket over my head, seeking refuge from the annoying sense of dread that has engulfed me. But as I lay there cocooned in my cozy sanctuary, a realization hits me like a ray of sunshine. Today is not just any day, Susie's picking me up in a few hours and in no time, I will be in Maple Hallow. I've got to get moving! If I want to have a tidy house before I leave, I'll have to peel myself away from this bed.

***

Susie will be here in five minutes, and I'm all set, except for one thing: I grab the untouched boxes of Christmas decorations I brought out in November and toss them back in the garage. No point in putting them up now. Just as I finish, my phone dings with a text from Susie.

Susie: Here! (smiley face, hand waving, and minivan emojis)

Me: Be right there!

I scamper back inside after shutting the door to the garage and snatch my small travel-size luggage—the one with the snowman pattern on it. It's been with me through thick and thin, and by that, I mean multiple airport mishaps and countless holiday trips. I still remember the time I stumbled upon it at a Christmas wonderland store in Switzerland during my college winter break. They had an array of Christmas-themed travel luggage covers, and I couldn't resist them. I bought five, but this one is my favorite.

Stepping out of my house, I'm greeted by Susie and Dave and their festive minivan. The cool air nips at my nose, and I smile at the beautiful winter day. It's one of those days where the sun is shining, the air is crisp and everything just feels right. Dave jumps out like a man on a mission, eager to get on the road.

"Hey there," he says, taking my luggage.

"Hi! Thanks," I say.

"You're very welcome," he says before scurrying off to the van like a busy little elf.

"Ready for our Christmas adventure?" Susie asks, her voice filled with excitement.

"Yes, I can't wait!" I reply, returning her enthusiasm.

I can't help but admire the reindeer antlers clipped to the car windows. "I love this," I tell her, pointing at them as I slip into the car.

"I knew you would," she says.

It's like finding a rare gem to have a friend who shares my love for Christmas. And Susie takes it to a whole new level by decking out her ride in holiday cheer.

As soon as I get into the car, Susie greets me with a compliment, "Cute outfit, by the way."

I grin from ear to ear as I reply with a heartfelt, "Thank you."

I couldn't decide what to wear today, my closet is like a winter wonderland, filled with Christmas sweaters. They may be called "ugly sweaters," but I think they're absolutely adorable. Today, I opted for a more subtle look, a white turtleneck with a tiny Santa Claus on the left, paired with my trusty jeans. To keep warm in the chilly weather, I layered a red puffer jacket over my outfit and slipped on my cozy snow boots. I made sure to pack some of my more outrageous sweaters for the rest of the trip.

"You too," I tell her. She looks absolutely stunning in her green sweater dress, paired with tights and boots. But the real show-stopper is the Christmas headband perched delicately on top of her head. And let's not forget the baby bump, which just adds to her already glowing appearance.

"Thanks," she says, with a little shoulder shimmy.

Dave slips in the car, mid shimmy.

"What'd I miss?" he asks.

"Eloise likes my outfit."

Dave laughs and shakes his head. "You're such a goofball," he teases, taking her hand and giving it a kiss.

Susie shrugs. "He thinks I'm crazy."

"Yeah, but you're my crazy and I love ya," Dave says with a grin.

I love how they complement each other so well. Even though Susie is outgoing and Dave is more reserved, they just work together. In fact, their differences are what initially drew her to him.

Susie always jokes about how they looked when they first met in college. She says she looked like a professor while Dave looked like a prodigy who got into college early. Even now at thirty-five, Dave still has that youthful appearance that could fool anyone into thinking he's still in college. He's got the kind of baby face that seems to defy the aging process.

Dave buckles up and backs out of my driveway as Susie cranks up the radio. Mariah Carey's "All I Want for Christmas" blasts through the speakers, and despite our terrible singing voices, Susie and I can't resist singing along. We drive with the same energy for pretty much the entire two-hour drive.

As we get closer, I notice the scenery changing around us. The trees stand tall and proud, reaching towards the sky and there's a dusting of snow on the ground. And as we climb higher into the mountains, the temperature starts to drop rapidly.

Looking out the window, I can see snowflakes slowly falling from the sky, coating the pine trees and the ground with a fresh layer of white. It's like the world is a blank canvas, waiting to be painted with the colors of Christmas. A proper snow event, or at least chilly weather, is a must for the Christmas season.

Dave slows down as the snow intensifies. "It's really coming down now."

I feel awestruck as I take in the view around us. "Isn't it beautiful?" I say with a smile.

Dave agrees. "Sure is."

Susie suddenly points. "Look ahead, Eloise!"

It's a bit dark now, since it's sundown, so I struggle to see what she's pointing at. I lean forward, squinting until it finally comes into view.

My heart swells with joy as I take in the sight before me. It's as if I've been transported to a winter wonderland, straight out of a fairytale. The town is alive with holiday cheer, and every street corner is adorned with twinkling lights and festive decorations. I feel a sense of childlike wonder come over me, and I smile from ear to ear. This is the Christmas town of my dreams, and I never want to leave.

The car is crawling along, but it still feels like he's driving too fast; I can't take it all in. *You'll be back, no need to panic, Eloise.* Before I know it, we're out of the town and heading deeper into the darkness. I turn back to take another look, but the town is just about gone, only twinkling lights are visible.

"That was magical," I say, breathlessly.

"I know. It always is. I love it here," says Susie.

"We'll be there in no time," says Dave, and he's right. We get to the cabin rather quickly.

Dave puts the car in park and he and I are the first ones to jump out. Susie is still inside, putting on her coat. I couldn't blame her, the wind was biting and unforgiving, and I was shivering despite my best efforts to stay warm. Dave hurries to the passenger side to get her door, but she's already throwing it open. He only has a chance to grab her hand to help her out.

"Let's get inside, I'll come back for the bags," he says.

"Thanks, honey."

I quickly follow them inside, so only a few flakes manage to land on my coat. Dave's holding on gently to Susie's hand, securing her every step. It's so sweet, it makes my heart melt.

As we approach the front door Susie turns to me and asks, "Are you ready to meet the Hall family?"

"Absolutely I am," I say, eager to meet them.

"Well, you are in for a treat," says Dave, opening the door for us.

This makes me pause, what does he mean? But before I can ask, Susie barges in.

"Mom," she calls out.

"Mike, they're here," I hear a woman squeal.

"Sweetheart, look at you," says a woman with the same squeal as before, and wraps Susie in a huge hug.

"Mom hasn't seen me in a total of two weeks," says Susie, turning to me. "It's a lifetime in mom years."

"Dave," she says next, and turns and embraces him in a similar hug.

"Mom, this is, Eloise," says Susie, smoothing her hair and taking off her coat again. "Eloise, this is my mom, Laura."

She pulls me into a hug too. "Eloise, what a beautiful name. Welcome and please make yourself at home. I've heard so much about you." Her sweet southern drawl adds to the warmth of her welcome.

"Thank you for having me, Mrs. Hall."

"Nonsense, call me Laura."

"Thank you, Laura."

"Come in, let's get close to the fire, it's freezing. Let me take your coat," says Laura, taking my coat and hanging it inside the coat closet. I take off my beanie and throw it in my purse.

Laura doesn't look how I imagined. Actually, I'm not even sure what I imagined, but she's far better than anything I could've dreamt up. She's got beautiful shoulder-length curls, with deep swirls of grey. A sweet southern accent that Susie didn't pick up and kind eyes that make you feel welcomed. Yeah, she's far better.

As we move from the foyer into the rest of the cabin, I'm in awe. I can't believe my eyes. It's a quintessential log cabin and even though I don't usually pay attention to architectural details, these are hard to ignore. My eyes are drawn to the tall windows and textured beams.

We enter another beautiful room, and my eyes are immediately drawn to the fireplace, flickering with warmth. As I look around the room, I notice an older man sitting by the fire in a dark leather chair, engrossed in a book.

"Grandpa," calls Susie, hurrying to the elderly man.

"Darling, you're more beautiful than ever," I hear him say.

She approaches him and says, "Grandpa, thank you! You're the best!" Then, with a playful grin, she turns to me and waves me over to join them. "This is Eloise, my bestie!".

"Hello, nice to me you," I say, shaking his hand.

"This is Grandpa Carl."

He looks at me with a warm smile. "Aren't you a beauty!"

I blush and thank him for the compliment, feeling at ease in his presence.

"Daddy," says Susie, walking past me, and hugging him.

"Sweetheart, your grandpa is right, you're glowing."

"Thanks. Daddy. Come," she says, turning toward me. "This is my best friend, Eloise."

"Nice to meet you, Eloise," he says, reaching for my hand.

"Nice to meet you, Sir."

"Mike, please. We're very informal around here," he says.

"You got it," I say, with a smile.

Mike's southern drawl is a bit lighter than Laura's, but just as warm and inviting.

After the hugs and introductions, Susie sits on the sofa, next to her mom and I join her there. Sitting next to her, I say nothing but observe how easy it is for her to be here, with her family.

I know we're not supposed to compare families, as we all come with our own set of problems and family drama. However, I can't help but notice how different Susie's family is from mine.

My parents are nothing if not formal. They're not about hugs or sharing Christmas with strangers in this way. Our Christmases are tame, quiet, and a bit lonely if I'm honest. My wandering mind hops back to the present and I pick up on Susie and Laura's conversation.

"Your brothers will be here soon," says Laura.

"Good. A storm is coming. I hope they get in before then," says Susie.

"I know, I'm just worried to death, you know?"

"I know Mom," they exchange a look I'm not sure I understand. "You can't worry your whole life."

"Tell me that after you have this sweet precious baby," she says placing a hand on her belly.

She places her hand over her mom's.

I feel a twinge of jealousy. I've always wanted to have moments like this with my mom.

"Hello," I hear someone say from the front door."

Laura jumps up from her seat. "He's here!" And in a flash, she's gone.

"My brother's here," says Susie, turning to me.

"I can't wait to meet him."

I contemplate waiting for her brother to enter before I ask where the restroom is, but truth be told, I've been holding it in for a while.

Can you point me in the direction of the bathroom?" I ask Susie.

"Sure, there's one in that direction." She points in the direction that we came in. "Or you can explore and go to one upstairs, there are three. You can also check out your room. It's the one at the end of the hall, to the right. You can take those stairs right there."

"Got it, thanks."

I decide to go upstairs and explore a bit. The cabin is not just cozy, it's exquisite and rustic. Upstairs, the cabin has a similar Swiss design, but with old country charm.

Turns out my visit to the bathroom was a smart one. My hair is a complete mess. I run my hands under the water and smooth my fingers through it. It's not perfect, but at least it doesn't look like I've just rolled out of bed.

"That's better."

With my makeup still intact, and my hair somewhat back in place, I head to what's going to be my room for the next few days, and when I find it, I'm not disappointed.

As I look around the room, I feel like I stepped into a Hallmark movie. Every detail is perfect, and my eyes can't settle on just one thing to admire. The soft candlelight casts a warm glow on everything, making the room feel cozy and inviting. And then there's the Christmas tree in the corner, decorated with white sparkling lights and ornaments, emitting the most glorious pine scent.

I can't resist sitting down on the plush-looking bed to test its comfort. As I sink into the mattress, I let out a sigh of contentment. Everything about this place is perfect. And although I never want to leave this room, I've been gone too long. I hear laughter as I reach the stairs.

It sounds like the room has exploded with joy. It must be her brother's arrival causing such happiness. I'm intrigued and excited to meet another family member. I pick up my pace until I'm back downstairs. It's hard to see him. His back is to me, plus, Laura and Mike are blocking my view. I approach Susie and wait for her to introduce us.

"Eloise, come meet my brother," she says.

I let her pull me toward him.

"Trev," says Susie, tapping his shoulder.

A shocked "Oh, no" spills out of my mouth.

CHAPTER 5

Trevor

I'm in my rental, halfway through Maple Hollow and they've really gone all out this year. I don't know how they've done it, but the town's Christmas committee has managed to add even more lights, decorations, and just more of everything.

I get through Maple Hollow quickly, and now I'm driving down a street covered in thick snow, and the pickup feels it. A short half a mile later, the cabin comes into view. I'm in complete darkness but for the lights coming from inside the cabin. It's truly a remote location. There isn't another cabin for at least a mile.

I pull in, park next to a minivan I'm sure belongs to Susie, and hurry inside away from the snow.

"Hello," I say, brushing the snow off my coat and

hair before fully entering. I'm not sure if they heard me, but then Mom is rushing toward me.

"My sweet boy! You made it," she says.

I'm already taking off my coat, in anticipation of her hug, which she wraps me in the moment she's close.

"Hey, Mom."

"I'm so glad you're home."

"Merry Christmas!"

"Merry Christmas, honey. Come, the others are by the fire." She puts her arm through mine leading me toward the others.

With every step their voices get clearer; Dad, telling Grandpa a joke he's heard before, Dave telling Dad that it was a good joke, Susie telling Dave he doesn't have to kiss up to Dad anymore, and Grandpa telling Dave he'll always have to kiss up to Dad.

"I'm home," I sing, coming into the room.

Dad greets me with his usual, "Hey son" and a pat on the back.

"Whoa, Susie, I didn't know you had a watermelon in there!" I joke, marvelling at the size of her growing belly. Susie chuckles, trying to get up from her seat but struggling a bit.

"I feel like a turtle on my back," she says with a grin.

"No need to stand. I'll come to you," I say quickly and rush down to hug her.

I'm gentle and barely touch her because I'm afraid I'll be too rough.

"I'm not made of glass, Trev," she says, sensing my fear, and standing.

"I know. I just don't know what to do with it." I straighten and look down at her, amazed by the fact that she's growing a human.

"Trevor, nice to see you," says Dave.

"Hey, you too, man." I shake his hand and turn to see one of my favorite people in this world, my Grandpa Carl.

"How are you doing, Grandpa?" I beeline toward him. He stands to greet me.

"Great, now that you're home."

I'm immersed in updates with Grandpa Carl, so I'm barely aware of my surroundings. But it's impossible to tune everyone and everything out. Dad takes a call, I think it's Chase, my little brother. As usual, Mom is speaking loudly trying to get Chase to hear her even though Dad's the one holding the phone. But even that didn't stop me from hearing one distinct sentence.

"Eloise, come meet my brother. Trev," says Susie, tapping my shoulder.

Finally, the moment I've been waiting for. When I turn, it takes no time at all for shock to spread over her features. It's none other than my Eloise standing in the middle of my family's living room.

CHAPTER 6

Eloise

This is not happening.

"This is Eloise, or should I say Dr. Eloise Parker," says Susie, standing between us.

He pauses and a trace of confusion crosses his face. I never told him I was a doctor. I bite my lip nervously hoping he doesn't give me away.

Then, he smiles that smile I remember all too well. "Yeah, we've m—"

But I catch him before he exposes us, or rather, me. "Nice to meet you, Trev, is it?" I fake it as best I can.

"Trevor, but I call him Trev," says Susie not picking up on my unsettled voice.

He gives me a sideways look, confused but

amused, as if to say, okay, I'll play along.

"Nice to meet you, Dr. Parker," he says, taking my hand.

"Eloise, please," I say.

"Okay, Eloise."

I grasp his hand, and he gives it a playful squeeze while flashing a mischievous grin.

"Honey, where do you want these?" I hear Dave say, and then Susie is off to help him with luggage, leaving us alone but for Grandpa Carl who's reading his book.

As I start to trail after her, Trevor reaches for my hand, pulling me back towards him. "Hold on there, Dr. Parker. Where do you think you're going?" he quips, the devilish grin fixed on his face. I glance over at Grandpa Carl, but I think he's completely oblivious to our little moment. "You're not getting away that easily," Trevor continues, giving my hand another playful squeeze. "So, we've never met? Judging by the shocked look on your face, I'm guessing you haven't forgotten me. So why keep us a secret," he says, still holding my hand.

I pull my hand away before anyone walks back in and sees us. I glance at Grandpa Carl again. His eyes are glued to the book.

"First of all," I say in a whisper. "There is no us. We met once."

"Fair enough. But I'm curious. Why did you tell

me you were a pastry chef?"

"Really? We need to talk about this right now?"

"When would you like to talk about it?"

"Fine. I don't know why I told you I was a pastry chef. People lie when they meet strangers, okay?"

"I didn't."

I hate that I lied and that I just admitted to it.

I can read his eyes. He's surprised, if not disappointed.

Truth is, I wanted to pretend I was someone else, for just one minute. I never thought things were going to go where they went. Then, it was too late to fix it.

"Anything else you lied about?" he asks, like his question bares no weight. Like I don't remember his pet-peeve about liars. I don't need to, but my mind does it anyway. It speeds through everything I told him back then. That was not the only lie.

"No," I blurt out because I just want this moment to end.

"Okay, I'll play along. I won't tell anyone about our time together. But to be fair, I'm not sure why. We're adults. We can do what we want."

"That's not the point. I just don't want Susie to know."

"That we were together or that you left without saying goodbye?"

"Never mind. I can see this is going to be too

much. Trevor, it was good seeing you again, and now I'm leaving."

I turn away and start heading upstairs, where I'm sure Susie is with my luggage.

"Eloise," Trevor calls after me, low enough for only me and maybe Grandpa Carl to hear. But I don't stop.

Thankfully he doesn't come after me. I have to leave. I cannot stay here with him. If Susie finds out that we...that I lied about so many things. No, I need to go before I'm completely humiliated in front of Susie's wonderful family.

I get to my room to gather my things, feeling sad that I only got a glimpse of what staying in this room would've been like.

I need a moment, so I plop down on the bed before I let the family know that I won't be staying. It's no surprise that thoughts of Trevor and me in a very different bed come to mind.

Six months ago, I was upset over the Chris fiasco and Trevor was in the right place at the right time. I'd like to say I didn't notice how cute he was right from the start, but I'd be lying. But he was more than that. He had a kind face and beautiful hazel eyes that showed a love for life I'd forgotten all about. Typically, guys like Trevor with a sleeve of tattoos don't talk to me, but he did.

When he said hi, and I looked up, I remember

thinking he was hot. He wore a loose black T-shirt that showed off his very defined muscles. I liked that it wasn't a muscle shirt. I appreciated that he wasn't trying to show off, it was just impossible to hide. He also had a light five o'clock shadow that didn't hide his chiseled face. The more we talked, the more relaxed and happier I felt. He made me forget not only about Chris but about the rest of my life.

He had an intoxicating vibrancy that drew me in from the first word he uttered. At a time when all I could see was ugliness, he was the embodiment of joy. I wanted more than anything for his joy for life to rub off on me.

As fate would have it, our connecting flight was delayed and eventually cancelled. But through every delay and setback, we were each other's constant companion. It was like something was bringing us together, slowly but surely, until we were inseparable.

Looking back, I don't know how I let things get so out of control. All I know is that I wanted to be someone entirely different than who I was. I didn't want to be the woman who let her boyfriend cheat on her. I didn't want to be the employee that hated her job. Or the daughter who let her parents run her life.

What started as two perfect strangers sharing a common dislike for flying and airports, ended up in a hotel room.

At first, it may have seemed that Trevor was

simply a means of revenge against Chris. Admittedly, that was initially a part of my reasoning. But as time passed, things changed between Trevor and me. It was like we were both searching for something, but not entirely sure what that something was.

The truth is, I was the one who initiated things with Trevor. In that moment, nothing else mattered but the fiery passion between us. The fact that we were practically strangers, or that our time together might be fleeting, didn't matter to me because when we kissed, I felt a rush of excitement I hadn't felt in a long time. And later, as we shed our clothes, I couldn't help but feel a glimmer of hope that maybe this could lead to something more.

But eventually I came to my senses and accepted the reality of our situation. We were two people caught up in the heat of the moment, with no real expectations for the future. And as much as I may have wanted it to be otherwise, I knew deep down that our time together was temporary.

That night with Trevor was like being struck by lightning— electrifying, intense, and impossible to forget. The passion we shared was beyond anything I had ever experienced before. In the two long years I've spent with Chris, I've never come close to feeling the way Trevor made me feel that night.

But now here we are, six months later, and I'm forced to face the consequences of my actions. I can't stay. I need to find Susie and say my goodbyes now.

As I approach one of the rooms, I start to hear faint chatter. It's Susie and Dave.

"Hey." The door is open, so I let myself in slowly, knocking while I enter.

"Hey," says Susie, sitting on the bed. She looks exhausted. Dave is unpacking their clothes.

"Listen, I don't think I'm going to stay."

"What? Why?" she asks, sitting up.

I haven't really thought through my excuse, so I blurt out the first thing that comes to mind.

"After giving it some thought I don't think this is a good idea. This is your family and I'm a perfect stranger to them. I can't impose on them during Christmas.

"Nonsense. You're my best friend, and everyone loves you and you're already here."

"I know, I just..." I struggle to find a rebuttal.

"Besides you can't go anywhere right now. Have you looked outside?" says Dave.

I'm confused as I look toward the window. Oh no.

"How did that happen so fast?" I say, unable to peel my eyes away from the window. "Wow, that's a lot of snow."

"Look at our van," says Dave.

I slide over to the right side of the window, to look for the minivan, and then I see it. It's covered underneath the pile of snow.

"Eloise, why do you really want to leave?" asks Susie. "Are you missing your family?"

"It's not that."

I don't know what to say.

"Please stay. It's only our first night here. Trust me, we're going to have a blast. You haven't even met everyone yet. My little brother and his girlfriend should be here soon. Well, with this weather, they might be delayed a little," she corrects, turning toward the window.

"I love your family. I'm not leaving because of them, but because of me."

"You'll be fine. I need you here with me. Please say you'll stay."

I turn my gaze back to the window and I am met with the sight of the blizzard raging outside. It's like the wind and snow are determined to keep me here.

For a moment, I ponder if I should tell Susie about me and Trevor, but I can't fathom the thought. She knows I'm with Chris. If I tell her what Chris did and that I've stayed with him during this entire time, what would she think of me? I scratched that idea immediately.

I can do this, I decide. It's only four days, Christmas will be here before I know it. I can keep my distance from Trevor and pretend he never happened. We can both try to be adults about this, and I'll try to enjoy my Christmas with his family.

One Christmas With You

"Okay. I'll stay."

"Good, let's go check out your room."

CHAPTER 7

Trevor

When Eloise turns away from me and hurries upstairs, I think, this might be the most interesting Christmas I've had at the cabin yet. I know I'm smiling, so I self-correct. I don't want to be insensitive. I could tell how nervous she was. She was practically shaking while I held her hand.

Grandpa Carl clears his throat, and I'm suddenly aware Eloise and I weren't alone. I turn and look over my shoulder. He's staring at me through the top rim of his glasses, his book sitting idle on his lap. I smile, hoping he hasn't caught on, for Eloise's sake. But I've never been able to pull a fast one on him, and I'm not starting today. When he casually nods back, I know it's too late. Ah Grandpa Carl, always one step ahead.

"I'm going to unpack," I tell him.

"Alright," he says.

I hurried upstairs after grabbing my bag and headed to my room. It's tucked in the back, at the far end of the hallway. I wanted to claim it before Chase got here because he's always after *my* room, especially since he's been old enough to bring his girlfriend home. Something about privacy, he goes on and on about. But this is my room—even though I no longer live here. A fact I have to remind him of.

There's one room downstairs and that's where Grandpa sleeps. Upstairs we have a total of six bedrooms. I reach the top floor and pass the first bedroom, Mom and Dad's. Then Susie and Dave's and, a few doors down, Chase's room. At the end of the hall is my room. And at the opposite end of the hall is the guest bedroom. That's where I assume Eloise is staying.

I go into my room resisting the urge to speak to her again. I decided she might still need a bit more time to get over the shock of seeing me after all this time.

This room only has the bare necessities: a queen bed, a small side table, and a standard dresser. There's a small pullout couch too because it's the only bedroom that has room for it. A week before we all show up Mom makes the switch to Christmas-themed bedding. The other rooms, she fills with decorations, including their very own Christmas tree. But, knowing that I prefer simple surroundings, she doesn't do the same in my room anymore. She wants me to feel at home, she told me once. The only Christmas thing in my room is the bedding. And that I can live with.

I'm unpacking the few items I brought and I'm folding them properly enough to make my mom proud. Frankly, I'm just trying to kill time and distract myself from what's really on my mind, Eloise. When that doesn't work, I give up and dump the remainder of my clothes on the bed. I take a seat next to them like they've beat me somehow.

I've grown used to not thinking back to that day with Eloise, but now, I feel the memory creeping in, and I don't fight it.

***

Six months ago, as I boarded my plane from Hawaii to Denver, I had planned on catching some shuteye, but things didn't go according to plan. I looked for my row, only to find Eloise already seated, in the window seat wistfully looking out. As soon as she sensed my presence, she turned to meet my gaze. Despite the hint of tears in her eyes, she mustered up a gentle smile.

"Hi," I said and took a seat.

Like everyone else on the plane, Eloise clutched her phone tightly in her hand. But as the announcement to turn off electronic devices echoed through the cabin, she quickly unlocked it and began scrolling through her texts. She started to type, but hesitated and quickly changed her mind. The brief moment spoke volumes about whatever was weighing heavily on her mind. As the plane began to taxi down the runway, she switched off her phone and stowed it away in her purse.

She seemed so upset I couldn't ignore it. At the very least I could offer some distraction from whatever was bothering her. Talking to strangers on planes is always tricky to navigate. Some people like to talk to make the time pass, but others refuse to even make eye contact. So, since she hadn't avoided me completely, I assumed she wasn't completely averse to chatting.

"Where are you headed?" I asked her.

"Georgia," she said, her voice a bit scratchy.

"Ah," I said, leaving out the fact that I was from there and that my entire family still lived there. This wasn't about me; it was about cheering her up.

"You?" she asked.

"Denver?"

"Oh, I like Denver."

"Yeah?" I wanted to dig for more details.

"Yeah, I've been a couple of times," she said, looking at me. I could tell she wasn't ready to stop talking. In fact, it seemed she welcomed my attempts.

"I'm Trevor."

"Eloise," she said, reaching for my hand. "Nice to meet you, Trevor."

"Nice to meet you, Eloise."

I was happy to see that the seat beside me was vacant. The empty seat meant that I could talk freely to Eloise throughout the flight without the fear of disturbing anyone.

***

The memory comes to a halt when Mom comes crashing in, already in mid-sentence with Dad following closely after her. I need to make sure I lock my door from now on.

Mom sighs and flops next to me. "Your brother can't make it here until the storm passes. God only knows when that'll be," she says. Her forehead creased with worry.

She has my full attention as I know what this means for her. She wants all her kids home for the holidays, but most of all, she wants them home safe. She likely won't rest until Chase walks through the door.

"Trevor, tell her it will be okay," says Dad, exasperated.

From the looks of it, Dad's been trying to reassure her to no avail.

"Mom, he's gonna make it and he's going to be okay. You have nothing to worry about," I say, putting an arm around her.

"Oh, I hope so. I think I'm going to start making some cookies to keep myself busy." She kisses my cheek and she and my dad leave as quickly as they came.

***

I'm finished folding and putting my clothes away when I detect the smell of cookies coming from downstairs. That was fast. Although she always bakes during Christmas, I know that tonight she's likely baking like crazy to distract herself from worrying about Chase. Wanting to make her feel better, I head downstairs to keep her company. But once I get there, I see Eloise has beat me to it. They're wearing matching Rudolph aprons, and they're moving about the kitchen as if they're in a baking competition.

"Smells delicious in here," I say.

"Told you these would draw them out," says Mom to Eloise.

"You did," says Eloise, glancing at me.

She quickly looks away as if afraid of getting caught.

As far as I'm concerned, the best seat in the house

now is right here by the island. The barstools aren't comfortable, but I don't care right now.

"What's in the oven?" I ask.

"Chocolate chip cookies," says Mom.

"And what are you making Eloise?" I ask, knowing that addressing her directly is bound to make her squirm.

"Um, I'm making sugar cookies," she says in a high-pitched tone, seemingly distracted by the ingredients in front of her.

She doesn't make eye contact with me, and I chew on my lip trying to piece together this puzzle.

She pours flour in the mixer and a small cloud of it explodes in her face. Some of the flour lands on her hair and she wipes it off with the back of her hand. In an attempt to clean herself up, she makes a small smudge on her face. But after a few tries she gets it all, except for a small smear on her chin.

"Don't worry Trevor, these will all be eaten," says Mom.

"I'm not worried," I say, with a chuckle.

"Well, I know how you feel about waste."

"You have something against cookies?" asks Eloise, briefly meeting my eyes. All pouring and mixing have stopped at once. This seems to be a serious question for her.

"Oh, he likes cookies just fine, he's just a minimalist. You know what that is?" answers Mom before I have a chance to.

"Yes, yes I do." Her forehead wrinkles with confusion as she seems rattled by this news.

"Is there something wrong?" I ask since she's still not moving.

But she doesn't answer me, instead, she asks, "What about Christmas?"

"What about it?"

"Do you buy decorations?"

"No."

"A Christmas tree?"

"No."

"No?" she repeats, stunned.

"No," I say, refraining from laughing as I can see this is very serious to her.

"I know, I know. We were just as shocked as you are when he made this transition," adds Mom.

"Mom, you make it sound weird."

"It is weird, honey."

"It's not weird at all," I argue.

"It's a little weird," mumbles Eloise getting back to pouring the batter and starting the mixer. If I could read minds, I would probably see hers spinning just like those blades. This news has shaken her. I don't know why. Or why it matters to her at all.

"Laura, where are the towels," calls Dad from upstairs.

"I swear if his head wasn't attached," says Mom,

hurrying to him without missing a beat.

Eloise and I are alone, and I feel like a moth drawn to light, my eyes lock on her taking in every detail. I watch as she squirms under my gaze, but she doesn't look up, instead, she pretends the mixer needs her full attention. I'm okay with that. It gives me the freedom to look at her. Every curve and line of her face seems to be perfectly crafted, like a work of art. She's even more beautiful than I remember.

The mixer comes to a stop, and she breaks her silence along with it, "Why didn't you tell me?" she says, spooning the dough onto the cookie sheet, finally looking at me.

"I didn't think it mattered."

"You didn't think it mattered. We spent twenty-four hours together, half of it I probably spent talking about how much I love Christmas and how much I buy during the season and the loads and loads of decorations I have but you didn't think it mattered to tell me it made you uncomfortable."

"I wasn't uncomfortable."

She rolls her eyes, not quite buying it. "Sure you weren't."

"Why are you so upset with me?" I say, catching her eye.

"I'm not," she says, putting the spoon down. "I'm sorry. I'm upset with myself. Seeing you here, brought back memories of how I behaved that day and, truth be told, I'm embarrassed."

Her honesty rocks me.

"Hey," I say, standing and moving around to her side of the island. "You have nothing to be embarrassed about."

We're standing close, and just like her, I have my own memories I can't shake, especially when we're this close. I get a whiff of her perfume and I'm right back at that airport, in that room.

"I appreciate you saying that, but I feel how I feel. I'm usually the responsible one. I don't do what we did."

"I know. You told me," I say, inching closer to her.

"You don't believe me," she says, her tone part question, part statement.

"I believe you. How can I make it better?"

"I don't know. I wish it hadn't happened. And I just want to enjoy Christmas and everything that comes with it even if that clashes with your lifestyle," she says, turning back to the cookies.

I lean back, next to the island, giving her space to work.

I grab one of the chocolate chip cookies, ignoring the comment about wishing we hadn't met. "Who says I don't enjoy Christmas?"

"How can you? You don't even have a Christmas tree," she says, sounding offended.

"Because Christmas is not about things," I say,

half-joking, trying to ease Eloise's mind. "It's about how you feel. Do I really need to remind you, of all people, the meaning of the holiday?"

She grabs the cookie tray and nudges me to move out of her way as she opens the oven door.

"Of course not. You just need to appreciate balance and understand that there's nothing wrong with bringing a little Christmas cheer into your home."

"Christmas cheer can happen in many ways, not just by buying things."

"Give me one example that's just as cheerful and magnificent as a decorated Christmas tree?"

"You."

"What about me?" she asks, shutting the oven door.

The one complaint my mom has ever had about her precious cabin is how small the kitchen is, and I've never been more thankful for it. Eloise is less than an arm's length from me and still is not close enough.

"Look how much joy you've brought to our family by simply being here. From what I can tell, my sister loves you and you're charming your way into my mom's heart as we speak. She doesn't let just anyone bake with her. You're better than any Christmas tree," I say, lifting my thumb to her chin, smoothing away the leftover flour with one gentle swipe.

I expect her to push my hand away, but she doesn't. Instead, she tilts her head with what seems like a beckoning look.

"Is it gone?" she asks.

"Yeah, it just took one swipe."

Recognition dawns on her face as I'm sure she remembers my thoughts about one thing, one experience being enough in most cases. A smile dances on her lips, but then it quickly disappears when Mom comes back into the room. Eloise jumps away, startled and I instantly drop my hand from her face.

"Okay, disaster averted. Your dad's got his towel."

Mom doesn't even notice us. She's right back where she left off, mixing ingredients to get the cookies finished.

Stepping away from this kitchen is the best thing I can do for both Mom and Eloise right now.

"I'm going to see what Grandpa's up to."

"Oh good, honey. He's probably trying to do something he shouldn't be."

I decide not to make Eloise feel uneasy in front of my mom, so I exit without saying another word or making eye contact. Even though I crave the chance to be alone with her, I'm willing to prioritize her comfort over my desires.

CHAPTER 8

Eloise

I'm in the kitchen in a frenzy because of Trevor. I'm glad he's gone. What was he thinking getting so close to me? Touching me the way he did? I mean I could slap myself right now. All he did was slide a gentle thumb across my chin and I practically melted like a marshmallow. If I'm going to survive this week, I'm going to have to be stronger.

Earlier, when I asked Laura if I could bake with her, I was uncertain of how she would react. I considered asking Susie her opinion, but she was resting, and I didn't want to bother her. So, I took a chance and asked Laura myself. Fortunately, she was delighted to have me join her. She kept chatting about how none of her children inherited her passion for cooking and baking, and how happy she was to have someone to discuss recipes with.

I hadn't baked anything in a long time, so I was a bit nervous when I started. But I knew exactly what I wanted to bake: sugar cookies. Although they're arguably the plainest cookies in the baking world, they hold a special place in my heart because they were the first cookies I ever baked. I've been perfecting the recipe ever since, experimenting with different techniques and ingredients to create the perfect balance of sweetness and texture.

The sugar cookies are out of the oven, and they look simply divine. A tantalizing aroma of vanilla and sugar has enveloped the entire kitchen, a comforting scent that seems to wrap around me like a warm blanket. Nothing evokes the spirit of Christmas quite like the sweet scent of baked treats wafting through the air.

I examine them carefully, making sure they meet my standards. The sugar crystals on top of each cookie shimmer like tiny stars, beckoning me to take a bite.

Suddenly, I am startled by Laura's voice. "Did they come out okay?" she asks, her expression reflecting a hint of concern. It appears that she has noticed my intense scrutiny of the cookies.

"Yes, I think so," I reply with a smile, holding up the tray for her to inspect.

"Oh yes," she exclaims, bouncing her finger on one of the cookies before taking a bite. "Look at that color. Golden brown edges, and soft." Her eyes lit up with admiration.

As she savours the flavor, a look of pure delight spreads across her face. "Whoa," she says, her voice filled with excitement. "These are delicious."

"Really? Not just any other sugar cookie?"

"Oh, no way. I've had plenty of sugar cookies in my day, and these are..." she pauses, turning the cookie around as if she's looking for the answer, "magnificent!"

"Thank you." I have to hold myself back or I might start crying. I think she notices.

"You love baking, don't you?"

"I do. Baking is my passion."

"I can tell, but aren't you a doctor?" she asks, confused.

"Yes, I am. I just like baking ...," I pause, "A lot."

"Well, honey, I'll tell you this. You only have this one life. Do with it what you want and don't waste one second doing anything else. Trust me. Life's too short to waste it on things you aren't passionate about."

Her easy-going response leaves me wishing I could get a similar reaction from my own parents. But there's no point in hoping for something that's never going to happen.

"Thanks again," I tell her.

"Don't thank me too much because I think I'm going to put you on baking duty this week."

"I would love that."

Her kind words lift my spirits momentarily, but reality sets in quickly. Baking is just a hobby for me, and I wonder if that will ever be enough.

For years, I've been weighing the pros and cons of quitting my job, but I just can't seem to make the jump. It's kind of funny, I've got a whole list of reasons to leave, but only a few to stay. Yet, those few reasons weigh me down like a brick tied to my ankle, dragging me under.

Firstly, I would no longer be making a difference. While not every patient I encounter is in a life-or-death situation, I have the opportunity to save lives when it matters most. It's an amazing feeling and quitting my job would seem selfish at the very least.

Secondly, I would feel like I had wasted all those years in med school. While I could argue that they weren't truly wasted, as I have gained a lot of knowledge and skills that I can use in the real world, it still feels like a waste to not apply my education to its intended purpose. I suppose I am similar to Trevor in that regard. I don't like to be wasteful, but for me, it's more about time than material things.

Thirdly, and perhaps most importantly, I would have to tell my parents. I know they would not accept my resignation and would ultimately guilt me into staying by reminding me of all the time and money they have spent on molding me. My mom would go on and on about what people would say and how I don't think about them at all. If my dad agreed at all, he would do so by demanding all the money they spent on me—not that he needed it, but for the principle of it. Which I could only repay in my dreams. These three cons keep me stuck and probably will for a long time.

It takes some convincing, but Laura agrees to let me help wash the dishes. I need this task more than she knows. As I start, I imagine that every dirty dish I soap up is a problem I'm washing away.

I grab the mixing spoons and pretend to wash away the issues with Chris. I decided then and there that things needed to be over between us. I'll break up with him as soon as I return home, maybe even sooner. I place the pan in the dishwasher and let out a small sigh as if I have just ticked something off my to-do list.

I pick up a bowl and begin scraping off the dried dough, but it's not coming off easily. I decided to let it soak for a minute, just like I was letting my career soak in uncertainty. As I reach for the mixing blades, I find that the dough is also stuck to them. I place them in the bowl to soak until they loosen, and it reminds me of my parents, cold, stiff, and unwilling to budge.

The cookie sheets, on the other hand, come clean easily, and it makes me think of Trevor. Maybe I'm making things harder than they need to be.

I would be lying if I said I'm not surprised by the news of Trevor's lifestyle. As I see it, being a minimalist seems restricting in so many ways.

I'm a little bummed if I'm honest. But why? Why do I care whether he gets a Christmas tree or not? I find myself heading down a rabbit hole of Trevor-related thoughts when I am abruptly brought back to reality by Laura's voice.

"Could you please check if the fire in the fireplace is out, honey?" asks Laura. "I'll finish putting away the rest of the dishes."

"Sure," I reply, turning to leave. But before I do, I say, "Laura, thanks for tonight."

"Of course, and remember, you're going to be my baking partner this week," She smiles, and it reminds me of Trevor.

I removed my apron and hung it back on the hook where I found it. Whatever warmth I had felt in the kitchen seemed to have left my body the moment I entered the living room. As I glance over at the fireplace, I see that the fire has indeed died out.

"I've got more firewood," says Trevor from behind me, holding an armful of logs.

"Trevor, my God. Can I help?" I ask.

"Nope, got it," he replies, as he moves past me

into the room.

I step aside but remain close by just in case Trevor needs my help. However, I know he won't. I can still picture what he looks like under that sweater, and I'm certain he could carry much more than just a few logs. I had merely asked to be polite, and now that I've thought of him naked, my cheeks flush with warmth. I quickly try to distract myself by expressing concern over the state of his clothes.

"Trevor, you're covered in snow. What were you thinking?" I ask with a hint of amusement in my voice.

"That we needed fire," he responds with a mischievous glint in his eye.

I raise an eyebrow and say, "Well, you could've asked for help, you know."

Trevor takes a beat before turning to me with a sly grin. "Wanna help?"

He moves closer to the fireplace and begins arranging the logs inside. I settle down next to him but remain silent. We fall into a rhythm, taking turns adding logs to the fireplace. Without any conversation, the silence between us becomes heavy, like the snow that has me trapped in this cabin.

As we work together, my mind wanders to the tension that always seems to be present when we're together. It takes all my willpower to not glance over at him.

I sense his eyes on me and suddenly he speaks up,

breaking the icy tension between us. "So, how have you been, Eloise?"

Trevor crumples a few pages of newspaper and tosses them into the fireplace, using them as tinder. He grabs a match and lights it, igniting the paper.

At the sound of my name on his lips, I pause, as memories of our time together flood my mind, leaving me feeling both nostalgic and uneasy.

After a brief moment of uncertainty, I stood up and took a step back, putting some distance between us. "I've been well, thank you," I reply flatly, unsure of how to engage in conversation with him. Every word that comes out of my mouth seems either too formal or too distant.

Despite my uneasiness, I continue. "And, I guess I haven't said it yet, but I want to thank you for hosting me. Your family is just lovely," I say sincerely. A small sigh of relief escapes me as I relax, dispelling the tension between us.

"Thank you. That means a lot," he replies, his voice steady and unchanged. His gaze remains fixed on me, and I can't help but wonder how he manages to stay so composed.

He stands up and begins to walk towards me, ignoring the distance that I've purposely put between us. Despite my efforts to keep him at arm's length, he seems determined to bridge the gap.

"What are you doing?" I ask, my eyes locked on

his.

"Why are you so nervous?" he responds, a mischievous grin spreading across his face.

"Trevor, stop it," I say, trying to hide the smile that's creeping onto my own face.

"Stop what? I just want to know why you seem so jumpy. You weren't this nervous when we first met," he teases.

"Please, it's not normal for two strangers to be standing this close to each other. Someone is going to notice."

"I'm not that close. And, we're not strangers, Eloise," he replies, his tone playful and light-hearted.

In truth, he's not that close. I know it's my paranoia making me feel like he's closer than he should be. But still, I don't want to risk it. The kitchen incident was too close a call.

"I already told you I don't want anyone to know about, well, you know," I whisper.

"I already told you I'm not going to tell anyone. You don't trust me?" he says, bringing a hand to his heart.

"I suppose I do." And I don't know how but I just know at my core that I can trust this man.

"Okay then, stop being weird, and let's just enjoy this together as new friends," he says offering me his hand in a truce.

The corners of his mouth quirk up and I give him

a curious look. Are we really doing this?

"Okay," I say, feeling my shoulders relax.

He's still holding my hand when Laura comes in. "I've got cookies and milk," she says, carrying a tray.

He drops my hand and steps back before she notices.

Within moments, everyone's joined us, and they're all reaching for cookies and milk.

I tear my eyes away from Trevor and move over to Susie, trying to appear unaffected by his presence. But despite my best efforts, my body betrays me, and I can feel my cheeks growing warm.

As I try to compose myself, a sense of unease settles over me. Being around Trevor again feels like too much, and I'm worried that my emotions will get the better of me.

Thankfully, no one seems to notice my discomfort, not even Trevor. He's making eye contact with everyone except me. I slip out of my wandering thoughts when I hear Susie's voice.

She plops down on the couch and says, "Trevor, you have to try these sugar cookies, no offense Mom, yours are amazing as always, but these..." she says, taking a bite and reaching for another.

She's tried these before, and dare I say, they're her favorite.

"No offense taken, they are scrumptious," says Laura with a warm smile in my direction.

Trevor inches closer, his hands rubbing together in anticipation. "Let's do this," he says, reaching for one of my freshly baked cookies.

I'm nervous, I can't help it. I want him to like them. No, scratch that. I want him to love them.

I'm trying not to watch him, but I can't force my eyes to look away, so I stop trying.

Finally, after what felt like an eternity, Trevor breaks the silence. "You're right," he says, his gaze meeting mine. "One of a kind."

I couldn't help but grin. It was a small victory, but one that left me feeling proud and accomplished.

"Told ya" says Susie, and then turns her attention to Laura. "Alright, spill the beans, Mom! We all know what's coming up this week, but Eloise here needs the rundown!" She winks at me mischievously, and I chuckle.

The rest of the family settles into their respective spots. Dave perches on the armrest of the couch next to Susie, while I take a seat next to her, putting some much-needed distance between myself and Trevor. Grandpa Carl sits back in his recliner, a contented smile on his face, while Laura and Mike cuddle up on the loveseat. Trevor remains standing and is back to avoiding eye contact with me.

Laura clears her throat and begins. "Tomorrow, we have to buy the Christmas tree, shop for food and a few more decorations. Since Trevor has the pickup truck, it's his job to grab the tree. Eloise, I figured you could go with Trevor that way you're fully emersed in our most special tradition."

"Now honey, are you sure that's a good idea? You know Trevor and his Christmas issues," says Mike.

"What issues?" asks Trevor, with a chuckle.

"I just don't know if you're the guy to help spread Christmas cheer."

"Because I'm a minimalist?"

Though he laughs it off, I see something different in his expression. Is he offended? Hurt?

She taps Mike's lap and says, "Oh honey, Trevor is perfect for this task. You're going to make sure she has a nice time. Aren't you honey?" She nods in Trevor's direction, making sure he's on the same page.

"I'd be happy to," he says with a seductive wink in my direction. I can feel my cheeks turning pink again, and I quickly avert my gaze.

Trevor's wink goes unnoticed by the rest of the family, but his gesture manages to make my heart race and my thoughts spiral out of control. Admittedly, I feel a twinge of excitement and nervousness. *Don't go down this road again, Eloise*, I tell myself. You cannot make the same mistake twice.

"Eloise," says Laura turning to me as if making sure I'm following.

I jump when I hear my name.

"You okay?" asks Susie, laughing.

"Oh, yeah, sorry. I'm fine," I assure her with a faint smile, although inside, my thoughts are still in disarray. "Yes, that sounds wonderful." Although I'm not entirely sure it does. An entire afternoon with Trevor, alone...

My eyes travel to him and he's not really in the room anymore, not mentally anyway. He must sense my staring, so he looks at me and offers a nod as if to say it's going to be okay. Funny what a simple nod from him can do. My heartbeat no longer feels like it is crashing against my chest. The ride has ended, and I'm coming out of it. Exhilarated but a little dazed and confused.

Meanwhile, Laura continues sharing her plans for tomorrow. "Mike and I will go shopping for the food. And, Susie, if you're feeling up to it, you and Dave can grab the decorations. I know how much you love doing that."

"Oh, I'm up for it, alright," says Susie.

"Dad, you can come with us if you like," says Laura to Grandpa Carl.

"Nope. I'll stay right here reading my book," he says, not even giving it a second thought.

"That's what we thought, just wanted to offer. You know you're always welcome."

After Laura finished going over everyone's responsibilities for the next day, we called it a night and retired to our respective rooms.

As I closed my eyes, I couldn't help but feel conflicted about my upcoming outing with Trevor. Was I dreading it, or looking forward to it? After some contemplation, I decided I was definitely looking forward to it.

CHAPTER 9

Trevor

By the time we finished planning for the next day, it was nearly 11 p.m. and most of us were beat. Eloise left for her room when Susie and Dave decided it was time to go. Right after that, Grandpa left too. Chase never made it in, but he called and said he would arrive tomorrow. After hearing this, Mom and Dad finally went to bed and so did I.

Sleep has completely eluded me, as I am unable to rein in my racing thoughts—all of which are fixated on Eloise. Eventually, I surrender and allow my mind to revisit our brief, but unforgettable encounter.

Six Months Earlier

We had been on the runway for about an hour when we were finally allowed to disembark. Getting off the plane she asked, "How long do you think we're going to be delayed for?"

"Who knows? But we should make the best of it."

"What do you have in mind?"

"Let's not sit around here. We gotta eat, no?"

She nibbled her bottom lip, considering my proposal. Although we had spent four hours in each other's company and had gotten to know one another to some extent, we were still strangers. I couldn't fault her for being cautious. However, in the end, she agreed.

"I am pretty hungry," she said.

"Good! I know just the place."

I was happy she was game because I was enjoying her company and wasn't ready for our time together to end yet. I had lounge airport access and though I didn't usually take advantage of it, I wanted to this time.

"Wow aren't you fancy?" she said, entering the lounge.

"Not really. My business card comes with some perks. It only takes one."

"One what?

"One card. One thing. One experience to make a difference. If it wasn't for this one card, we'd be out there, eating questionable fast food," I teased.

"Thank God for your one card," she said with relief.

During the next few hours in the lounge, we took the time to get to know each other better over a meal. I learned that she used to travel overseas a lot, primarily in Europe, with Switzerland being her preferred destination. She shared her passion for Christmas and the numerous boxes of decorations she owned. I also found out that once she feels comfortable with someone, she is quite talkative, which I didn't mind in the slightest. It was intriguing to see how she navigated indecisiveness, such as when the waiter came to ask if she wanted a drink.

"Should I?" she asked, a twinkle in her eye.

Little did I know it was a rhetorical question, as she had all the answers and follow-up inquiries ready.

"Well, probably not," she said. "But perhaps just a glass? One can't hurt, right?"

I was amused and ready to respond when she carried on, her words tumbling out like a playful stream.

"But one will lead to two. No, no thank you," she told the waiter. But before he got too far, she said, "One. Just one, right?" This time she waited for an answer.

"One is all you need," I said.

"Okay, one glass of red wine, please."

"And a beer for me," I added.

A single glass of wine caused her delicate features to relax, and the lines of worry on her forehead faded away. She was vastly different from the woman I had met on the plane just a few hours earlier.

I didn't think the wine was entirely responsible for this change. Sure, she was chattier after the wine, but I was a good listener, which had put her at ease. I was glad that she felt comfortable talking to me, and I enjoyed listening to her, but not for the reason she thought. I liked watching her, but I played it cool, as I didn't want to frighten her or come across as creepy.

She was stunningly beautiful. Her blue eyes, and long lashes, captivated me the moment she met my gaze. Despite her hair being a bit disheveled and her makeup smudged, she radiated a natural beauty. There was a refreshing authenticity about her that was irresistible. I was undeniably drawn to her.

I listened closely as she spoke about being a pastry chef. In hindsight, it's so weird that this was all a fabrication. I suppose we all have our reasons for why we embellish certain aspects of our lives, I just don't know why she felt she had to. I'd given her no indication that I wanted her to be anyone other than herself.

A few hours later, we received the news that our

flight had been cancelled and we would need to book another. It was already midnight, and neither of us felt like boarding another plane. So, we decided to book the next available flight for the following day and stay close to the airport. We made our reservations and took a shared taxi to the hotel. However, when it was time to go to our separate rooms, she invited me to hers.

***

December 23rd

It's bright and early the next day and judging by the silence, I'm the first one up. Though I slept great, like I always do, I can't say the moments leading up to sleep weren't frustrating.

Today's trip to Maple Hollow has my thoughts in a whirl! This is going to be the first time Eloise and I will be alone again like we were six months ago. Though she's made it plain that she has no intention of revisiting our past and wishes to banish it to the forgotten realms of time, I eagerly anticipate spending time with the girl I met back then. The one that isn't afraid to look at me or talk to me. The one that doesn't fidget when I get too close, as adorable as it might be.

I've already checked the weather to ensure that

our plans are still a go! It's a chilly 10 degrees Fahrenheit with a sprinkle of snow, but I was fully prepared for this. As long as I can dig my trusty truck out of the snow, my day with Eloise is all set!

I finish slipping into my jeans and a sleek black sweater and step out of my bedroom. That's when I spot her, coming out of her room. I shut my door, but paused for a moment, drinking in the sight of her.

She's also dressed in jeans and a sweater, but she looks so much better! Her sweater is a fiery red, with a dazzling Christmas tree at its center, twinkling with lights. It's the perfect attire for someone who loves the holiday season as much as she does. As I stand there, admiring her, she catches my gaze and stands a little taller, radiating confidence.

"What better way to get into the festive spirit than with a sweater like this?" she chirps, a smile spreading across her face. "I'm ready to go find the perfect tree!"

I wonder if she's had a change of mind. Maybe she realized that having met me six months ago isn't the worse thing my family has ever heard. As dismissive as I might have been toward her request, I do understand. I know it's not the actual meeting that she worries about, it's what happened that she wants to keep a secret.

"It's perfect," I say.

We step forward at the same time and we pause,

as if there's not enough room for the two of us, only there's plenty—too much if you ask me.

"Ladies first," I say, allowing her the space she needs.

"Thank you."

She takes the stairs ahead of me, and as she passes, the scent of sweet vanilla swooshes by me and it's like I'm back in that hotel room.

Now at the bottom of the stairs, I drive any thoughts of that night away. "Would you like some coffee?" I ask her.

"I'd love some, thank you."

I follow her straight to the kitchen, where she takes a seat at the island, exactly where I sat last night.

It's my turn to be on display and so I busy myself with coffee-making.

"Can I ask you something," she asks, curiosity dripping from her voice.

"Sure."

"Your dad doesn't approve of your lifestyle?"

"Guess not. You mean last night, right?"

She's perceptive.

"Yeah, couldn't help but notice his comment bothered you."

"It didn't bother me. I just didn't want my mom getting upset about it. She's been through a lot. Besides my dad is just upset because I'm not an exact replica of him."

"I'm sure that's not true."

"Sure it is?" I say, grabbing two Christmas mugs from the cabinet.

"Trevor, be serious," she insists.

"I am," I say laughing again, which does little for convincing her of my seriousness.

"You're not. I remember this about you."

Her eyes squint a little in my direction as if she's just figured me out, or she's trying to recall something.

Now she has my full attention.

Coffee is brewing so there's no need to stay an island apart. I walk around to stand closer to her.

"Oh yeah, what exactly do you remember? Wanna take a stroll down memory lane?" I tease her knowing how incredibly uncomfortable this question will make her, but I can't help myself.

"Stop it?" she says, looking over her shoulder.

I move back slightly, just enough to not cause any attention if someone were to walk in but still close enough to take in her scent.

"I'm just playing?" I tell her.

"I'm trying to be serious?"

"Let's back up for a minute. What do you remember?" I ask her again.

"That you're always joking about everything."

"Being serious is overrated."

"Can you just try for a moment?"

I play along, but not in the way she wants me to, "Anything for you Eloise."

She rolls her eyes at this because she doesn't love sarcasm, at least from what I remember.

"When you said your mom's been through a lot, you meant because of what happened to you?"

"I don't want to be the cause of any more pain for her," I confess, briefly caving into the seriousness she needs.

"I can tell you're a good son. You know that, right?"

I don't really know how to answer or what she's expecting from me. I manage to give her a sliver of what I hope will satisfy her by nodding.

"Trevor, your car accident, was just that, an accident. You can't blame yourself for what happened, you know, dying, and coming back," she says, in a whisper as if even I shouldn't hear it. "And if you are, then you shouldn't. Be grateful for the fact that you healed yourself. I mean, how amazing is that?" she says, with more enthusiasm than I feel it deserves. "If you're holding on to guilt, if this is why you've selected a life of minimalism, then you should set yourself free, you've done nothing wrong?"

"That's not why I'm a minimalist," I tell her, surprised that she's come up with this assumption.

"Isn't it though?"

I'm not even close to understanding where she's

going with this, but I'm pleased that she's at least talking to me.

Our alone time is cut short once again by Susie and Dave.

"Morning," they say.

"Good morning," says Eloise, startled.

I guess she's not quite comfortable being alone with me after all.

"Morning," I say, and turn to watch the slow-brewing coffee.

Before the coffee's done, the kitchen is packed with family members.

"Is everyone ready for today? Oh, it's chilly out there," says Mom, joining us too. "Morning, sweetheart," she says, squeezing my arm.

"I'm ready," says Dave.

"Me too! Eloise, are you excited?" asks Susie.

"Of course," she says, glancing in my direction to check if I'm listening.

"Mom, this is Eloise's first time in Maple Hallow, can you believe it?"

Mom is throwing on her apron and doesn't miss a beat. "Honey, you're going to just love it. I wouldn't be surprised if after today you don't make plans to move here and leave city life behind," she says, grabbing the eggs from the fridge.

"Mom, Eloise would never."

Eloise isn't saying much, just observing the

conversation these two are having about her as if she's not even here. I'm amused, and I think she is too.

"Why not?" asks Mom, addressing Eloise directly.

Eloise is about to respond, but no chance she's getting in a word before Susie.

"Because she's a doctor in one of the biggest hospitals in the country," says Susie, scrolling on her phone, and handing Mom a spatula. How she manages to multi-task so easily baffles me. "Besides Eloise isn't the kind of person that makes decisions like that, am I right?" she finishes, turning to Eloise waiting for an answer this time.

"Well, I—"

"See, I told you," says Susie.

Eloise doesn't fight her. It's like Susie knows her better than she knows herself.

"Well never say never," says Mom.

Eloise nods, agreeing with Mom, or Susie, not quite sure. But what I am sure of is that it's time to make breakfast. As usual, Mom begins assigning breakfast tasks. I'm on toast duty as everyone's afraid of my cooking. And even this isn't a good idea. I've managed to burn toast plenty of times.

Mom makes the best eggs and hashbrowns, so she never relinquishes that job to anyone. And though Susie is typically the one who creates the perfect tablescapes, today Mom has ordered her to sit and stay off her feet. So Dave is doing the bare minimum when it comes to setting the table. One plate, one fork, and one napkin—which I totally appreciate. Eloise offered to make pancakes from scratch, and Mom was very excited about it.

Grandpa Carl's at the table sipping orange juice and reading the same book from yesterday. He will have no part in the "breakfast shenanigans," as he puts it. Grandpa is a simple man, with little need for things. Maybe that's where I inherited my gene for minimalism. He doesn't like to fuss over things and wants no one to fuss over him. He wants to be around us, when he's good and ready, and has no problem leaving us—even if it's in the middle of a game. If he's had enough stimulation, he puts himself first.

Now, sitting around the breakfast table we chat casually about the weather, Chase being trapped, and our plans for the day. I'm half tuned in when I hear Mom addressing Eloise.

"Eloise, you're going to have to write a cookbook," says Mom, after taking a bite of the pancake.

"I know, right? Mom, I have so many of her recipes. Part of my weight gain, even before I got pregnant, is her fault."

"You're too kind, thank you," says Eloise, blushing but proud.

"You cook with your whole heart, I can tell," adds Mom.

"I try," she says, and her eyes light up and then

quickly dim.

No one picked up on the subtle shift in her expression or the way her voice fluctuated when she spoke, not even Susie, which surprised me given their earlier interaction, but I noticed.

"These are the best damn pancakes I've ever had," adds Grandpa.

"Thank you," she brightens even more at his compliment.

Something tells me she knows Grandpa is the quiet type and not prone to offering compliments. I'm impressed that she managed to engage him. I have to see what these pancakes are all about.

I poke two with my fork and bring them to my plate. I don't douse them with butter or syrup, like I normally would because I want to taste them—really taste them.

"Trevor, make sure you pick out a nice big tree. Don't skimp. I want a healthy one that's not going to shed the first day we get it," says Mom.

"I will," I say with a mouth full. And once I'm done chewing, I agree with the rest of the family, "These are the best pancakes I've ever had Eloise... really."

We give each other a two second glance. The corners of her mouth lift in a tender smile. In that moment I understood why she told me she was a pastry chef. Sometimes the only way to be who we want to be is to say it out aloud to someone who might just believe it.

After breakfast, bundle up is the buzzword as we get ready to go into Maple Hallow. Mom can't believe that all I brought was the coat I'm wearing. She wants me to wear a scarf and gloves and a beanie, which I refuse while reassuring her that I'm fine.

Eloise is completely bundled up, but the cold is bitter, and it shows on her cheeks. I've already started the truck hoping to warm it up before she gets in, but my plan fails. I open the car door for her and it's still freezing inside.

As we pull away from the cabin, leaving the others behind, Eloise is already seeking the warm air from the vents, eagerly thawing her hands over them. I sneak a peek at her, taking in the tiny sigh that escapes her lips as we drive away. Her eyes flutter closed like she's basking in the moment before she suddenly grins at me. I'm left wondering what's going on in that beautiful mind of hers. If only I could read her thoughts!

CHAPTER 10

Eloise

As we leave the family behind, I can feel his eyes lingering on me, but I play it cool and pretend not to notice. There's just something about him that has me all twisted up inside like I'm back at the airport and under his charming spell once again.

To survive this week, I've come up with a new narrative about him: like, he's not my type. Sure, he's handsome, a head of dark hair and a stature that's the perfect height, and kind and a good listener but then there's the matter of those sleeve tattoos and his inability to take anything seriously. I mean, I can't exactly bring him home to meet the parents with all that ink on display.

What am I talking about? Meet my parents? What

am I even thinking? I never understand my own thoughts. I smile at him, grateful that he can't read minds.

"Want some music?" he asks.

"I don't think you'll appreciate what I want to listen to," I say.

"Let me guess, holiday music?"

"Of course. Is there something else one should listen to during Christmas time?"

"I guess not," he says with his usual grin and then turns on the radio.

Trevor wears a permanent smile on his face as if he's privy to a joke that nobody else understands. It's as if happiness just naturally flows through him, leaving a trail of joy in its wake. How does he do it? How does he maintain such a light-hearted demeanor?

"You don't have to," I say reaching to change the station.

"Eloise," he says, placing a hand over mine. "I like this music too. I don't mind."

I quickly pull my hand away from his, as if his touch is too much to bear.

"Sorry," he says, his eyes focused on the road ahead as he grips the steering wheel tightly.

Shoot!

"No, I'm sorry," I stammer. "I didn't mean to do that."

"Why did you?" he asks, his voice laced with curiosity.

Typically, he'd make a witty remark, and I'd reciprocate. But this time, his question caught me off guard. As the town comes into view, I don't want the rest of our tree shopping trip to be filled with awkwardness. I shake my head at myself, why do I always have to overthink things?

"I don't really know. I... I guess I just wasn't expecting it," I admit.

It's only half the truth.

"Fair enough," he says simply.

The other half of the truth is that his touch, even if it was just a brief one, takes me back to that fateful day when we met. And I refuse to let myself dwell on it because if I'm being honest, I've thought about that night countless times since then. When I thought I'd never see him again, I could live with what I did - even though it was completely out of character for me. But now that he's back in my life, everything has changed. I'm glad he doesn't press for more because I'll just have to pile on another lie.

As we make our way into Maple Hallow, I'm enchanted by the quaint, charming town. The daytime might not have the same charm as last night, but it still holds a certain magic in its own way. I take in the various stores and sights that line the streets, savoring each moment. I know there's no rush to see everything all at once, and I'm content to bask in the beauty of this place for as long as I can.

Once we're close to the shops, he finds a parking spot in the middle of the bustling town and we both get out. I watch my step because the last thing I want is to slip and fall.

The winter day ahead of us is a scene straight out of a postcard. Not a single cloud dares to obscure the sun, and the wind remains calm and still. Despite the sun's warm rays shining down upon us, I can't seem to shake off the chill in the air.

"So, the tree shop is down at the end of the street?" he says, pointing.

But I'm awestruck once again. "This is absolutely perfect," I say, looking around.

He notices my wandering gaze, and he takes in the town as well. "Yeah, I suppose it is, especially for first timers," he says. "Come on, we can stop and look at whatever you want."

We cross the street to the sidewalk lined with little shops and I'm relieved to find that the snow from last night's storm is not a slushy or icy mess. We're surrounded by twinkling lights and Christmas wreaths adorn each light pole. Across the street, a man's melodious violin playing captures the spirit of the town and the holiday season with every note. I find myself stopping in my tracks, mesmerized by the beautiful music.

"He's amazing, isn't he?" Trevor asks, a hint of a smile on his lips.

I'm completely entranced by the violinist's performance and can't tear my gaze away. "Incredible," I respond.

"He's here every year and he takes requests. Do you have a favorite song you'd like to hear?"

Not wanting to impose, I hesitate to make a request. "I couldn't."

But Trevor insists. "Why not? He's here to spread joy. I know you must have a favorite song."

I feel like a kid on Christmas morning, eager and giddy.

"It's The Most Wonderful Time of the Year," I finally tell him.

Without missing a beat, Trevor takes my hand and leads me across the street. "Come on."

Together, we wait patiently for the violinist to finish his song, then Trevor puts in my request.

Even though I can't see my goosebumps, I can feel them. They form on my arms the moment the song starts.

"This place is amazing. I can't believe I've never been here," I confess, without tearing my eyes away from the violinist.

"Don't you live close by?"

"Yes, since I was six!"

"Oh, I guess I assumed you were from here.

Where are you from?"

"Originally, New York."

"Oh," he says, as if he's just figured something out.

"What?" I say, knowing what he's about to say.

"I think I get it," he says as if he's just solved the puzzle. "Eloise. Like *Eloise at the Plaza*," he says, grinning.

"Yep." I stiffen and pretend I'm not affected. But it's written all over my face that I don't think it's as funny as he does.

When I was little, in school I shared that my mom named me after a popular book character, they didn't think it was as charming as I did, and I quickly learned to keep that story to myself. However now, for those who are familiar with the book, and subsequent movie, I don't need to tell them, they already know.

"Touchy subject?" he asks.

"Do you mind, I'm trying to listen." I step forward, away from him.

In typical Trevor fashion, he steps forward too, not giving me the space I obviously need.

"So is *Eloise at the Plaza* a big theme for you?"

"Maybe," I whisper not taking my eyes off the violinist.

"I love it," he says.

"Sure, you do."

"I think it's adorable."

"I'm sure you do," I say, and take another step

toward the violinist and away from him.

This time he doesn't follow. Finally. Now, I can listen to the song in peace.

Judging by the growing crowd that's formed since we got here, I'm not the only one that loves this song. It should be the anthem for the holidays.

Glancing over my shoulder, I search for Trevor, half-expecting him to have disappeared into the crowd. But he's right where I left him. As our eyes meet, he winks as if to say, I'm not going anywhere.

As the final notes of the song fade away, the small crowd begins to scatter, and I find myself drawn back to Trevor's side. Without a word, we seamlessly continue on our journey, just as we were before the enchanting performance of the violinist.

"Thank you for that," I finally say, breaking the silence.

"My pleasure."

"It is a touchy subject, the *Eloise at the Plaza* thing," I confess.

"Sorry, I didn't know. I wasn't trying to pry."

"I'm just surprised you didn't ask me when we met. Everyone always asks. I liked that you didn't."

"Honestly, I'm surprised I didn't."

"Me too," I say, laughing.

As we make our way down the sidewalk, the soft strains of the violinist's music still linger in the air. It's a beautiful gift he's given the town and I'm grateful to be a part of it. Just as we're about to cross another small street, Santa's sleigh comes into view, and families with their children are gathered along the road, eagerly awaiting his arrival.

"Look," I point as if Trevor's somehow missed it. He hasn't of course.

"The kids love this part. I've volunteered a few times, serving hot cocoa, or giving directions. I've done and seen it all, but this by far is the best thing here."

"You volunteered here, really?" I ask with utter shock.

"Why are you so surprised?"

"I don't know."

"Back to the minimalism thing."

"I suppose. I just don't get it."

"It's okay. Most people don't."

We never stop to watch Santa engage with the crowd, but I do look back and sneak another look because it feels like I'm in a fantasy and everyone's playing along. I haven't felt this much in the spirit since I was a kid. No matter how much I've tried to recreate those first few Christmases, with holiday music, decorations, and all the baked goods, I haven't been able to do so. But this. This is it.

We cross the street again and pass a charming coffee shop called Mrs. Claus' Coffee. It has a long line stretching out the door and I totally get the waiting for coffee thing. I've been known to wait in a coffee line more times than I care to admit.

"Have you noticed the Christmas-themed names of the shops around here?" Trevor asks, pointing to the bookstore with its sign reading Letters from Santa. Then I noticed the deli named The North Pole, the corner shop called The Gingerbread House, and a bar named Scrooge. "Grandpa Carl and Dad made all of these signs at their shop," he adds.

"They did?"

"Yeah, they do things like this all the time?" "Carpentry is basically their whole world," he says, with a hint of sarcasm.

"Does it bother you?" I ask, observing the subtle change in his demeanor.

"Nah, not at all."

But I can tell from his expression that there's more to the story. I don't press him, sensing that he's not eager to delve deeper into the subject. Instead, I turn my attention back to the signs, admiring their intricate details. "They're truly magnificent," I remark, meaning every word.

"Indeed," Trevor nods, "Maple Hallow's success may be a year-round affair, but its roots and prosperity stem from the holiday season. To keep the tradition alive and not become complacent, they always try to bring something new to the table each year. This year, it was these festive signs."

"I love that," I say, admiring the effort the town puts into keeping the spirit of Christmas alive. Trevor's smile grows wider. "I knew you would."

Moments later, we arrive at the Christmas tree place, also known as Santa's Village, and I feel overwhelmed by the multitude of options. Trevor seems to pick up on my hesitation.

"Don't worry. I've been doing this long enough to know the good trees are not at the front," he says, taking my hand, leading me to the back of the tent.

As we make our way through the maze of evergreens, I realize that my approach to finding the perfect Christmas tree is to simply let it choose me. I've never been one to have a specific type in mind, I prefer to simply let the tree that speaks to me be the one to take home. And as we wander through the sea of green, I find myself drawn to a certain tree, as if it's calling out to me. I know, without a doubt, that this is the one.

And just as I was about to speak up Trevor says, "This one," pointing to the very tree that caught my eye.

"Yes. It's perfect."

"Excuse me, over here!" Trevor calls out, beckoning the salesman.

"Be right there," he replies, his voice ringing out from across the tent.

As we stand guard over our newfound tree, we

watch as other shoppers flock to the front of the tent, settling for less-than-perfect specimens. But here in the back is where the truly magnificent trees reside. Trevor's instincts were spot on.

"I think we can safely let go of the tree now," Trevor says, observing my tight grip.

I let out a laugh and released the tree. I'm confident that no one will be stealing it from us.

"We did good," he says, extending his hand for a high five.

"Definitely," I agree, giving him a satisfying slap of my hand against his.

But then we fell into a weird silence far longer than I cared for. As we wait for the salesman to return, Trevor starts to get restless.

"Where did that guy go?" he says, scanning the aisles.

"Your guess is as good as mine," I say, looking around.

And again, stillness descends upon us but this time I fill the silence by opening up about a subject that I wasn't entirely certain I was ready to discuss.

"My mom loved Christmas before I was born and right up until I turned six. *Eloise at the Plaza* had been a favorite of hers. That's where I got my name," I tell him, even though he didn't ask.

"What happened after six."

"I don't know. I never asked. All I know is that we

stopped going to the Plaza. And then my mom stopped loving Christmas."

"She doesn't celebrate it?"

"My parents do, but as far as I'm concerned, it's no different than any other dinner party they host. Sure, there are Christmas lights outside and a giant tree, but that's about it. There's no Christmas spirit."

"Why haven't you asked?"

Before answering I contemplate the question, to make sure what I know to be true, still stands.

"I don't want to know. She stopped loving Christmas, but I didn't. Those are some of the fondest memories I have, and I don't want them tarnished. I'm selfish, right? Something awful could've happened and because I don't want Christmas' to be ruined, I can't bother to get to the bottom of what happened."

"You're not selfish. It's your life and you have the right to choose how you want to remember it."

Before I get a chance to tell him how refreshing his response is, the salesman finally shows up.

"So, you want this one right here?" He confirms.

"Yep," says Trevor.

In a flash, he grabs the tree and whisks it away.

We're supposed to follow, and Trevor starts to but before he gets too far, I reach and grab his arm.

"Hey, one second. Thanks for saying that. You always know what to say to make me feel better. I remember that about you too."

"Anytime, Eloise," he says stepping toward me.

I stood rooted to the spot. It seems I had initiated an invitation. Our bodies were closer than they should have been, closer than I had wanted them to be when I learned that he was here. Yet, as he inched closer, I found myself unable to push him away. Instead, I stood firm, grounding myself in the moment.

CHAPTER 11

Trevor

At first, I don't even hesitate when she grabs my arm. I don't need to take a step toward her, but I do. Our foreheads are now touching, and with her lips inches away, I yearn for a kiss. Eloise bites her lip, and I know where this could lead.

"Why did you leave without saying goodbye?" I ask the one question that's been haunting me for the past six months.

"The truth?" she asks cautiously, mindful not to disrupt the closeness between us.

"Always," I reply.

"I don't know," she says, her voice barely above a whisper.

I don't believe her. I think she knows exactly why she left and I don't know why she won't just tell me. Unlike her, I now feel myself slipping away.

"We should go," I say softly.

She takes a step back, her gaze averted. "Yeah, we should," she says, fidgeting with her coat as if trying to smooth out imaginary wrinkles. "Our tree is waiting for us," she adds.

I smile, but it feels flat.

She returns a hesitant smile before turning away again.

"Eloise, wait," I call out.

She pauses, looking back at me. I want to tell her that if she doesn't trust me enough to be honest with me, that we have no business kissing. But I don't say any of it, because today isn't supposed to be about me, or what I need. It is about showing Eloise around Maple Hollow and getting a Christmas tree.

"Never mind, after you," I say, instead.

She nods with a small smile, and we continue toward the front of the store in silence. We didn't speak to each other the entire drive back.

***

Once we got back to the cabin, we were greeted by the rest of my family who had already made their way back. Mom was overjoyed with our choice of Christmas tree, even without seeing it in all its glory, and thanked us for finding the perfect one. But despite the joyous atmosphere, I noticed Eloise's retreat to her room, citing a headache. I knew better, though. She was upset, and I couldn't blame her. Our exchange at the tree shop probably left her feeling confused, just as her sudden departure from my life all those months ago had left me feeling the same.

Aside from the trust thing, there's still a lot of time to be spent with everyone here. Tonight, we'll trim the Christmas tree and everyone will be around, and I don't want Eloise to feel uncomfortable. During our trip to town, before I brought up the past, I saw a glimpse of the woman I met six months ago. I thought we could have a good time this week without so much awkwardness. If I had kissed her, I'm sure she would have regretted it.

As dinner time draws near, the aroma of our next meal permeates the cabin. As usual, Mom is in the kitchen, carefully crafting each dish with love and care. Meanwhile, Eloise has come downstairs but is keeping her distance from the rest of us, spending most of her time by Mom's side.

I'm sitting on the couch waiting for dinner and watching a game when Dad comes in.

"Good game?" he asks.

"Yeah, Broncos are up by seven."

"Oh yeah, forgot you're a Broncos fan now."

"Not now. For ten years."

"That's right, I also forget you went there for college."

He didn't forget, he just never got over my decision to go to school in Denver instead of his alma mater. Or my decision not to come back and join the family business. He never understood that carpentry wasn't my thing.

The situation only became more challenging after my accident. He had anticipated that my decision to leave the finance industry was a sign that I had finally come to my senses and would return home. However, when I announced my plans to open a gym, the disappointment was palpable, crashing down upon me like a huge wave.

"How's the gym going? Is business good?" he asks.

I had intended to wait until after the holidays to tell him, but it seems like that's not going to be possible now. Maybe he's already run out of disappointment and will simply support my decision. I mute the game, and as I do, Grandpa Carl walks in, giving me an audience of two as I deliver the news.

"I sold the business."

"You did? When?"

"Just last week?"

"Why?"

"I'm wanting to do something else?"

"Like what?

As the heat crept into the cabin earlier, I decided to shed my long-sleeved shirt for something a little lighter. So, when I leaned back and lounged with my hands behind my head, my sleeve tattoos were on full display. I couldn't resist a little bit of mischief, knowing how much Dad disapproved of my body art. But, hey, maybe flaunting my tattoos would serve as a gentle reminder that my latest announcement wasn't as shocking as the time I showed up for Christmas with my arms covered in ink.

"Travel." I finally announce with a grin, ready for his reaction.

"Oh, for heaven's sake," he exclaims, rising to his feet and waving his arms in frustration.

"Laura, come in here!" He calls out.

"Let the boy live his life," Grandpa interjects with a supportive smile.

"Stay out of it, Carl," Dad scolds, annoyance clear in his voice.

I return Grandpa's smile, grateful for his unwavering support. As for Dad, well, he's always been this way, upset with every decision I make.

"What's going on?" says Mom, as she quickly surmises what just happened. "Oh no, you told him?"

"He asked about the business, what was I supposed to say?" I'm half laughing now.

"Wait, you knew?" Dad asks, sounding surprised.

"Honey, he told me weeks ago. He asked me not to say anything because he wanted to tell you himself."

"Great, now you've got my wife keeping things from me," Dad says, throwing his hands up in frustration.

"It's not that serious, Michael," says Grandpa.

"Not that serious?" yells Dad.

Everyone is now in the room, including Eloise, who senses that this might be a family matter and hangs back, keeping a safe distance.

"What's the buzz, folks?" chimes in Susie, as she enters the room.

"Your brother is throwing his life away, that's what's going on?"

I'm still chuckling, my feet kicked up on the table and arms behind my head, waiting for the storm to pass. I know Dad's going to give me a good talking-to, but I'll just have to wait it out.

"What is it now?" asks Susie.

"So you've thrown away your livelihood by selling your business and now you plan on meandering aimlessly through Europe like a naive teenager?" He sneers, fixing his gaze upon me.

"You did?" asks Susie.

"Everyone just calm down. It's Trevor's decision. He knows what he's doing," says Mom.

"Still, Europe? You're not going to be here when the baby's born? She's your first niece!"

"Susie," I sit up, my heart heavy at the sight of her being upset. "We can stay connected through Facetime. I won't be gone forever," I assure her, and I'm taken aback as my gaze inadvertently wanders towards Eloise.

Why I felt the sudden urge to glance in Eloise's direction, or why I was so invested in her opinion on my travels, is a mystery to me. But all I can say is that for the very first time since announcing my grand adventure, I'm starting to think maybe I should've stayed put for just a little bit longer.

"Alright, alright, let's put this behind us and enjoy the remaining time we have together," says Mom.

"Okay, but you better keep your word and come visit us the moment you step foot back in the good ol' US of A," says Susie with a playful grin.

"I promise," I say.

After the semi-truce, Mom bustles back to the kitchen, with Eloise hot on her heels. Meanwhile, Dad makes a hasty retreat upstairs to be alone. This is just his way of processing things. We all know it and respect his space. He needs time to deal with things in his own way, and I can relate—in many ways, I'm just like him. Susie goes back upstairs, leaving me and Grandpa alone.

I reach for the TV remote, ready to unmute the volume and immerse myself in the game, but Grandpa puts a halt to my plans.

"One day, my boy, I pray you stop running."

"Grandpa, I thought you had my back!" I protest playfully.

"I always have your back, but I'm not blind."

I pause for a moment, considering his words. Was I running from something? The thought had never crossed my mind, but now that both Grandpa and Eloise have hinted at it, I can't shake the feeling.

CHAPTER 12

Eloise

I'm trying my best to bake the Christmas cookies I promised Laura, but it's been difficult to concentrate after witnessing Trevor and his dad's argument. Trevor didn't truly argue, he just sat there with a half-smile, seemingly unaffected by his dad's words. I don't want to judge, especially when all I could think about was how good he looked in that black T-shirt. When he wasn't looking, I took a quick glance at his arms and noticed a few new tattoos. It's frustrating that I remember his tattoos, but they're just so hard to forget.

I'm whipping up a batch of delicious peppermint chip cookies. Susie mentioned that they were Trevor's favorite and, before I could even think about it, I found myself offering to bake them.

Laura's pantry is a dream come true for any baker. With shelves stocked full of ingredients, including flour, extracts, spices, and every utensil and cookie cutter imaginable, I had everything I needed. I set up my station at the end of the kitchen island, away from Laura's cooking station, where she was humming "Jingle Bells," seeming to have put the earlier argument behind her.

I am still somewhat shaken by the argument, but my mind is mostly occupied with thoughts of our trip into town today. I know that we almost kissed, and it would have been my fault, just like the first time. However, he always says and does the right thing, always considering how I will feel later. I am aware that this is what happened at the tree shop, but I was still deeply embarrassed, which is why I immediately went to my room after we returned.

Six months ago, he did the same thing. He tried to warn me, but I didn't listen. Trevor understood the potential for regret and guilt. But I was persistent and didn't want to think about the consequences of my actions. I didn't want to be responsible or cautious or worry about how I might feel later. And it was great at the moment. But then I woke up afterwards filled with guilt.

Although Chris had been unfaithful to me, I was not like him. I valued loyalty, and that night with

Trevor I strayed from my values. I should never have let things go that far. And, I should have told Trevor that I was in a relationship, he deserved to know. Especially since I got the sense that he wanted more for us. And strange as it may sound, secretly, I was hoping for more too.

For all these reasons I ran away like a coward, sneaking out in the middle of the night after having spent the best night of my life with him. Yeah, Trevor was right not to kiss me today.

He probably thinks I'm a mess. One minute I want to pretend we don't even know each other, and the next I'm practically throwing myself at him.

The truth is, I haven't been the same since that night. For the past six months, I've constantly wondered what could've happened if I hadn't run away from that hotel room.

It's taken me six months to finally come to terms with what I need to do about my relationship with Chris. The guilt has become unbearable, and the thought of being touched or kissed by him is now unthinkable. I need to put an end to things.

Laura's cheerful hum of "Jingle Bells" has been ringing through the air and I hum along as I make my way back to the pantry, searching for a set of holiday-themed cookie cutters I spied earlier. Just as I'm about to return to my station, Laura's keen eye catches my selection.

"Ah, these are my favorite," Laura coos, as I stand before her with the basket of cookie cutters.

"They're just so adorable," I reply, admiring the collection.

Laura approaches, with a gentle smile.

"These were passed down from Mike's mother," she shares with a hint of nostalgia.

"Wow, these are so unique. It's like the new ones just can't compare," I muse, still sifting through the basket.

"Exactly, let me show you." She plucks a few cutters from the basket until she finds the one she's looking for. "This one was used the first time Mike brought me home to meet his parents."

I hold the metal Christmas tree cookie cutter in my hand, examining the small handle that's perfect for pressing down on dough.

Laura smiles, her eyes twinkling as she tells me her story. "I was so nervous back then," she admits. "But I loved baking and so did Mike's mom. She invited me into her kitchen that first Christmas and we baked together every year after that until she could no longer do so."

I gaze at the piece of metal, imagining all the Christmases it's been a part of, and the memories it holds. The thought of someday sharing something similar with my own family fills me with warmth.

"Thank you for sharing this with me," I say,

appreciative of the history that's been passed down. Laura nods, tapping my hand softly.

"I knew you would appreciate it," she says before returning to the soup she's been cooking.

I focus my attention back on the cookie dough and carefully begin cutting out shapes with the special Christmas tree cookie cutter. As I work, my thoughts drift back to what had Mike so upset and the nagging feeling that's been bugging me since then. Trevor is leaving the country, but why? For how long? I shouldn't care. It's not my business and it doesn't affect me in any way. Yet, I can't shake this inexplicable feeling that's been gnawing at me.

As I carefully shape the cookie dough into festive Christmas trees with the vintage metal cutter, I wonder if my stories of travel had any impact on his decision. But then, I shake my head and remind myself not to be so arrogant. Surely, I couldn't have had that much influence on him. Yet, as I continue shaping the cookies, a small smile tugs at my lips at the thought that maybe, just maybe, I was more than just a fleeting encounter to him.

As I'm finishing up the last batch of cookies, everyone comes into the kitchen. The moment I see Trevor, my hand slips and the cookie cutter drops onto the floor.

"I'll pick that up for you," Trevor offers.

But I respond too quickly, "No need, I've got it," I

say with a hint of nervousness that doesn't go unnoticed by Susie, who raises an eyebrow. "Thanks anyway," I add, trying to mask my unease with a smile.

Trevor shrugs his shoulders, playfully raising his hands as if to say, "no problem," and finishes with a cheeky wink that only I see.

CHAPTER 13

Trevor

The mouth-watering scent from the kitchen lured us all in, and it's unclear if it was all of us or just my appearance that made Eloise drop a kitchen tool. Her nerves were palpable. I wish she could just let go and see that even if my family found out about us, no one would judge.

"I knew it was just a matter of time," Mom chimes in as we all gather in the kitchen.

"Sweetheart, you know how irresistible this kitchen becomes when you start cooking," says Dad.

Thankfully, Dad's mood has improved. Just before we all gathered in the kitchen, he even helped bring in the Christmas tree in preparation for tonight's tree decorating.

As Susie approaches the stovetop, Mom lifts a pot, and the delicious scent of dinner wafts through the air. Meanwhile, Dad joins Dave and Grandpa Carl at the dinner table, where they begin discussing the details of their next carpentry project. It's no surprise that the conversation turns to their favorite subject, especially when seated at the dinner table, a true masterpiece built by Grandpa himself.

Despite being officially retired, Grandpa still spends a lot of time in the shop. I'm surprised he hasn't snuck away to work on some projects.

The carpentry business was once Grandpa's before it became Dad's. He brought Dad on board even before he married Mom. Growing up, I always heard that the business would one day belong to Susie, me, and Chase. When I was young, Chase and I were open to the idea, but Susie was not so much. This didn't seem to concern Dad much until I announced that I wasn't going to follow in his footsteps. Before that day, I remember thinking that I could do this. Watching Dad and Grandpa create custom pieces, everything from furniture to music boxes, was truly a gift. There was something special about knowing that each piece of furniture was unique and created for one person, rather than mass-produced. This resonated with me, but apparently not enough.

As time went by, my interests evolved. I longed

for new experiences beyond what was familiar to me. This led me to pursue my education in Colorado, then a career in finance, later starting my own business, and now traveling to Europe. I often think about what my life would have been like if I had stayed in one place like my family did. I probably wouldn't have been involved in that car accident that almost took my life.

The accident remains a hazy memory, both distant and ever-present, tangled in the fabric of time. I can't shake the feeling of that fateful night, no matter how hard I try. It's a part of me, ingrained in my soul like the tattoos etched onto my skin.

I was driving home from work one Friday night, after putting in a late shift to catch up on some long-overdue paperwork. My job wasn't far from home, so I usually took the quieter back roads. But on that night, I was tired and wanted to get home faster, so I took the highway.

The memories of that night remain cloudy, with only snippets of recollection returning to me. I was told that I was a mere mile away from my exit when a drunk driver crashed into me, causing my car to flip over multiple times. The next thing I remember is waking up in a hospital room, groggy and disoriented, with the doctors breaking the news to me that I had technically died, but they managed to resuscitate me.

My parents flew out, and with every word the

doctor spoke, I could see the pain etched on my mother's face, her heart breaking as the reality of what had happened hit her.

The accident weighed heavily on me, even though it wasn't my fault. I constantly questioned what could have been done differently. What if I had left work just a moment sooner? If I had never ventured out to Colorado for college, or if I had simply listened to my dad's wishes and taken up the family business? Would I have been spared from having to experience that? These thoughts plagued me, even though I knew deep down it wasn't my fault.

Snapping back into the moment, I playfully address Eloise. "Baking up a storm again, I see!" I aim to add a light-hearted tone and let her know that everything's cool.

"Yes, your mom invited me to bake something for us and I never turn down a chance to bake."

"Eloise dear how are you liking that cookie cutter?" asks Mom.

"I love it," she answers with a quick glance my way. Eloise gives me a defiant look as if to let me know she's not bothered by my presence. But just as quickly as it appears, her gaze drops, and she looks away.

I survey the room and see that everyone is wrapped up in their own activities, with Mom and Susie stirring pots on the stove, and the guys absorbed in their carpentry chat. This presents a prime opportunity for mischief!

Eloise is so focused on cutting out her cookies that she doesn't even realize I'm sneaking up behind her. I lean in, my words a playful whisper. "What are you whipping up today?"

She startles a bit, but I steady her with a light touch on her waist. I don't want to draw any attention from the others.

"What are you doing?" she asks eyes wide.

"I wanna talk," I reply, still keeping my voice low.

As Susie momentarily steps back from the stove, Eloise shoves me back with her elbow. But Susie's not looking our way. She and Mom are having a conversation about Braxton Hicks contractions, so they don't notice our interaction. I take the opportunity to move closer to Eloise and lean against the kitchen island next to her, trying to look casual as if I'm simply interested in what she's baking. Our conversation remains intimate and private, thanks to our proximity.

I owe Eloise an apology for earlier. I acknowledge my role in the situation. "I'm sorry about what happened earlier."

"There's nothing to be sorry about. We were both caught up in the spirit of Christmas. Let's forget it ever happened," she says, busying herself.

"I wasn't caught up with Christmas." She looks up,

meeting my gaze. "I was caught up in you."

As we stand there, our thoughts tangled in the possibilities of what could have been, Eloise's breath quickens. But just as we're lost in the moment, Susie's voice breaks in, pulling us back to reality.

"Trevor, you are going to die when you taste these peppermint cookies," yells Susie from across the kitchen but already making her way to us.

I move aside, because I might be a little too close for Susie's liking.

"Well, you know peppermint cookies are my favorites."

I tighten my jaw as I reluctantly move away from Eloise when what I really want is to whisk her away to a private space where we can be alone.

Susie is now across from us on the island, her forearms resting comfortably. She looks like she's stretching more than actually leaning on the island.

"Of course! Why do you think Eloise is making them? When I told her these were your favorites, she offered to bake them."

I flash a grin, delight spreading through me. I'm sure Eloise wanted to keep this between them, but Susie has let the cat out of the bag. It's a small gesture, but it means a lot to me.

"Is that so?" I say playfully to Eloise.

Her face reddens instantly.

"Yes, I wanted to express my gratitude for

showing me around town today," she says, her gaze fixed on the cookie tray, her voice suffused with a hint of nervous energy.

I've stumbled upon a familiar quirk of Eloise's, the way her voice raises and quickens when she's nervous. It's a tell sign that has come back to me now.

"Well, then I'm going to have to return the favor somehow. After all, you showed me a thing or two about Christmas," I say, with a playful grin.

"Just be nice, no pranks," Susie warns.

I raise three fingers in salute and place my hand over my heart, "Scout's honor, no pranks."

Eloise turns to me, and her cheeks are flushed with color.

"Susie, be a dear and grab the rolls from the oven," calls out Mom.

And just like that Susie's back at Mom's side tending to the rolls. I take the opportunity to walk away too. I've made Eloise nervous enough for one day.

***

It's tree trimming time. We're gathered around the tree—except for Grandpa Carl, who's resting on the recliner shouting out instructions on how and where we should start.

Mom divvies up baskets overflowing with Christmas ornaments, while she and Eloise scurry off to the kitchen to retrieve the sweet treats Eloise baked. Meanwhile, Chase's arrival remains a question mark, with his flight once again delayed. He promises that tomorrow, he'll finally make it home.

We have the perfect Christmas ambiance going, with the fire crackling, snow lightly falling outside, and the sweet scent of peppermint in the air. Dave is in charge of the tunes, and after a momentary hiccup with Google finding the right station, it finally comes through. Susie gives Dave a high-five when her favorite song, "White Christmas" by Nat King Cole, starts playing first.

"Cookies anyone?" asks Eloise.

With a beaming smile, Eloise strides into the room, cradling a platter of freshly baked peppermint cookies. Mom trails behind, balancing another tray with small glasses filled to the brim with cold milk. The tree trimming comes to a halt as we set down our baskets of decorations and gather around the coffee table.

Eloise hangs back, observing our reactions to her delicious creations as the rest of us eagerly dive in.

As I take a bite of the cookie, I'm met with a burst of flavor that exceeds my expectations. Mom was right, Eloise bakes with her heart and soul. The deliciousness of the cookie has me under its spell, and I'm completely absorbed in the experience. So much so that I'm hardly aware of Eloise until she starts to share the secret ingredients that make these cookies so good.

"I've always found that using white chocolate chips instead of milk chocolate enhances the peppermint flavor," she says, with a touch of hesitation. "And, it's important to be careful with the extract. Too much can overpower the taste. It's all about finding that perfect balance."

It's cute the way she describes her process.

"They're perfect," I say, turning to her. "Best peppermint cookies I've ever had."

"Thank you," she says with a smile revealing an inner spark that had been hidden until this very moment.

A smile spreads across my lips as I admire how beautiful and proud she appears at this moment. I quickly finish my last cookie before returning to trimming the tree. However, I don't make much progress before Susie pulls me aside. She eyes Eloise carefully, as if she doesn't want her to overhear our conversation. Eloise remains oblivious, engrossed in sorting through the ornaments and singing along to the song playing in the background.

"Trev, do you have the ornament?" she whispers, and I realize I almost forgot about it.

"Ah, yeah, it's right over here," I respond, leading her to the mantel where I left it earlier.

Susie joins me, her eyes gleaming with

anticipation. "I'd like to take a quick peek before giving it to her."

"Sure thing," I say, handing it over.

I hand her the small box and her expression says it all. She's beyond happy with my attention to detail.

"You bought a box for it? You're the best! You dork." She hugs me a little longer than the gift calls for and I sense there's something wrong.

"Hey, you okay?" I say, returning her hug, but pulling back to see her face.

"I'm just worried, you know?" Her eyes are filled with tears she's trying to hold back.

"Sus, I'm going to be okay. Besides, I'm just a phone call away. It's no different than me living in Colorado. And if you ever need me, I'll hop on a plane, you know that, don't you?"

"I do, I do. Don't mind me, it's just these hormones, they have me feeling so much," she blew an aggravated breath and composed herself fully before peeking into the box.

"This is beautiful," she says, glancing inside. "C'mon, let's give this to her."

Once we're next to everyone again, Grandpa is shouting commands at someone. It takes me but a second to see that his target is Eloise.

"Here?" she asks, placing an ornament against the tree.

"Lower," he says.

"Here?" she asks again, having moved the ornament to a different section.

"Higher," he says, glancing at us with a wink.

"Grandpa, leave Eloise alone," says Susie, sparing her from any more teasing from Grandpa.

"Alright, alright, that's perfect," he says, chest twitching with suppressed laughter.

"Lend me your ears, oh beloved kin," Susie calls out.

The whole family stops what they're doing, their eyes all trained on Susie. I take a step back, my arms folded across my chest, giving Susie the spotlight.

"Eloise come here," she says.

Eloise delicately places the ornament that Grandpa's been teasing her about onto the tree, then sets the basket down. She approaches Susie with caution, unsure what to expect.

"What's going on?" she asks with concern.

"Eloise, I wanted to get you something special to show you how grateful we are that you're spending Christmas with us," says Susie, her voice ringing with excitement. "I asked Trevor to pick this up for you. Consider it a little token of our appreciation and love. Merry Christmas!"

Eloise's lips curve into a warm smile. "This is so kind of you. Thank you." She embraces Susie with one arm, while her gaze settles on me.

"Open it, open it," urges Susie.

Eloise carefully removes the lid, revealing the ornament inside.

"Merry Christmas, Eloise," she reads the inscription on the ornament with a smile.

"Oh, let's see it," says Mom, standing next to her.

She holds the ornament up by its string, letting it spin in a mesmerizing circle. Her smile grows with each twirl, spreading from cheek to cheek.

The snowman glass ornament caught my eye immediately, and I knew it was the one. As I observed the other shoppers, I noticed a group of women gushing over it, further solidifying my decision. Without knowing it, this ornament was meant for her, and I couldn't be happier with my choice.

Eloise tucks the ornament into its rightful place among the others on the tree. She may not fully understand the significance of this gesture, but I do. This ornament symbolizes her place within our family, a cherished member who holds a special place in our hearts. With the final touch of decorations added to the tree, I took a picture to preserve the memory.

As the family retires for the night, Susie and Dave are the first to bid farewell, followed by Grandpa. Determined to do my part, I offer to clean up and secure the house for the night, allowing Mom and Dad to go to bed without worry. After a day of tireless service, Mom deserves it.

I lock the front door and make my way to the kitchen, where I'm greeted by the sight of Eloise savoring one of her peppermint cookies.

"Hey," she says, finishing her bite.

"Hey."

"Everyone went to bed?" she asks.

"Yeah, they were tired," I say.

I know I shouldn't linger around her, but the allure of being alone with her is too strong to resist.

"By the way, thank you for the ornament. It's beautiful."

"You're welcome," I say. She's standing in front of the island, and I step closer, never taking my eyes off her.

As she scans the kitchen, her eyes dart around as if she's cautious of any prying eyes. Then with her voice laced with wonder, she asks, "Why do you look at me like that?"

Uncertain of what she means, I ask, "Like what?" Still moving toward her.

Our eyes meet again. With urgency, she adds, "Like I mean something you."

Without hesitation, I respond, "Because you do."

But she shakes her head, dismissing my words. "I don't. I can't possibly," she asserts, with a small smile dancing on her lips.

As I move closer to her, the air around us crackles with electric tension. "I haven't stopped thinking about you for six months."

I am only inches away from her, and I can feel her breath on my face. The moment is charged with anticipation, and I can sense that she feels it too.

Surprised by my confession, she asks, "You haven't?" her voice barely above a whisper.

With unwavering confidence, I reply, "No, not for one single day. Can you honestly tell me you haven't thought of me?" I wait for an answer, but her voice fails her, and she can only shake her head.

The attraction between us has reached a boiling point and I find myself closing the small distance between us. A magnetic pull drawing us closer.

Inches from each other I have a choice to make. The most sensible option would be to step back and walk away, just like I did earlier. But that's not what I choose to do. Unexpectedly, she leans into me, and I cup her face in my hands. "From the moment I laid eyes on you again, I've been wanting to kiss you."

With each passing second, the urge to finally claim her lips becomes stronger. But still, I hold back, savoring the moment.

"We shouldn't," she breathes, but her lips already ghosting over mine. "We'll only complicate things."

I cannot resist any longer, and I give in to the desire that's been building between us. She tastes like peppermint, and I know in that moment that she and my favorite treat are forever linked in my mind.

I have no sense of space and time. The world around us fades into oblivion. We break our kiss for a split second. Another choice to make, walk away or keep going. Walking away is not in play for me. I lift her effortlessly onto the kitchen island because I want her to think of me—of us, every time she gets near it again.

We are locked in a fiery embrace, fueled by both ferocity and tenderness, a balance of power and gentleness that makes me never want to let go. Every second feels like an eternity, a blissful pause in time where nothing else exists but the two of us, but then I hear it. A breath. A sound.

"Trevor. Trevor." She says my name, and it takes me a minute to realize she's asking me to stop.

"Sorry," I say, pulling away from her.

I run my hands through my hair to keep from touching her. The only way to come off this high is to run outside in the bitter winter cold.

"I can't," she says.

"Okay, okay," I say.

Against every urge in my body, I step back another step.

"I'm sorry," she says, jumping off the island and walking out of the kitchen without looking back.

"Eloise," I call after her, but she's already gone.

CHAPTER 14

Eloise

I leave the kitchen in pure panic. I know that everyone's asleep, so I grab the keys to Dave and Susie's minivan, and I leave. Where exactly I'm going remains to be seen. I want to go back home, but I can't very well steal the minivan. Besides, what kind of friend would I be if I did that? No, I won't go home, I won't leave like this, not again. But I do need a minute to think, away from him.

It takes no time at all to make it into town and I still don't know where I'm going. Maybe I'll go to the pub Trevor pointed out earlier. What was it called? I remember it was tucked away in a corner. But at night, and from inside the car things look different so I can't quite pinpoint where I saw it. I'm driving up and down the streets hoping it just comes into view.

The late hour means most stores are closed, and I find myself wishing they weren't. Maybe I could have stopped in and killed some time, indulging in a bit of shopping therapy. I'm not sure if Trevor would approve of such a thing. In fact, I know he wouldn't. There's no doubt in my mind about it.

Despite my best efforts to distract myself, my mind keeps wandering back to him. It's like every street I turn down, every thought I have, leads me straight to him. I try to shake him off, but his presence lingers like a stubborn shadow.

He didn't forget about me. In fact, it's the opposite. He's been thinking of me, just like I have been thinking of him. No! Stop! Don't entertain this, Eloise. Even though I was embarrassed, he was right not to kiss me earlier. Ugh! Why did he have to kiss me now? And why did it feel so right? It feels like we're caught in some sort of twisted dance. He wants me, but I say no. I want him, but he says no. It's a frustrating game of tug-of-war.

As I cruise down a brand new street, my eyes light up like a Christmas tree as I spot it - Scrooge! I take my foot off the gas and ease on the brakes as I descend down a narrow road.

Pulling up to the pub, I can see that there are only a handful of cars parked outside, but who cares? It's open! I slam the car into park and take a deep breath, bracing myself for the bone-chilling air that's sure to send shivers down my spine.

I never bothered to take off my coat during the drive, so it's an easy exit from my car. I slam the door shut and hurry inside, eager to escape the biting cold. I quickly make my way past a beautiful brunette wearing the skimpiest of dresses, engrossed in her cell phone conversation. I wonder how she's not freezing in this weather.

My sudden entrance into Scrooge makes some heads turn in my direction, and I freeze. With a small wave, I say, "Hello," under my breath, trying to appear as unobtrusive as possible.

I get a few equally tiny waves, but I'm mostly ignored. Before I take my first step, everyone's turned back around.

As I take in my surroundings, it becomes clear why this pub is called Scrooge. The interior is devoid of any of the traditional Christmas decorations one might expect in this town. Actually, it could easily pass for a bar in any other town at any other time of year. The dim lighting casts a shadowy pallor over the entire space, creating a somber atmosphere. The only hint of festive cheer comes from a string of multi-colored lights, along the bar.

The bar itself is sparsely populated, with only a handful of patrons scattered throughout. They seem to be lost in their own thoughts, nursing drinks and staring off into space. It's eerily quiet, with the only sounds coming from the low murmur of conversation and the occasional clink of glasses being set down on the bar.

I don't want to take up an entire table, so I sit at the bar. The moment I do I'm approached by the bartender. "What are you having?"

"A glass of red wine, please?" He places a napkin in front of me and runs off to get my drink without saying another word. Nothing like the warm reception I've been getting since I got into town. The contrast continues.

The exhale that leaves my mouth is louder than I mean it to be, and now I've got the attention of the woman next to me. She looks at me for a beat, like she's weighing her options. Should she, or shouldn't she?

"Hi, you okay?" she asks, with a tilt of the head, sorting me out.

Maybe she's wondering if that glass of wine I just ordered is my first, or first of many.

"Hi, yes, sorry about that," I say, blowing out an even heavier breath.

"Don't worry about it. Hi, I'm Ava."

"Eloise."

"I love that. Are you from around here? Is that why your parents named you Eloise?" she says with exaggerated enthusiasm.

"Um, no. I'm originally from New York, But I've—"

"Oh my God, that's even better. You're like Eloise, *Eloise at the Plaza*."

I wonder if she grasps that this probably isn't the first time I've heard this. I want to tell her, but I don't have the energy.

"Yeah, just like that. My parents have a great sense of humor," I say, the lie of the century. When God created my parents, he forgot to give them a funny bone.

"Here you go." The bartender places my red wine in front of me and leaves as quickly as he comes.

Ava is seated a few stools away, and I can immediately tell that she is stunningly beautiful. She has the kind of natural beauty that doesn't require any makeup, but she still wears it nonetheless.

I'm discreetly eyeing her as I sip my wine when suddenly a guy approaches her. I'm about to get annoyed because I can predict the future. He'll probably use some lame lines to try and get her to leave with him. But then, to my surprise, I find out they're already together.

"Honey, this is Eloise, and she's from New York. Get it? It's like *Eloise at the Plaza*. Isn't that so adorable?"

"Hello," he says seemingly embarrassed for me.

He flashes a smile that shows off his deep

dimples. Under the warm glow of the bar's light, he looks like a young Johnny Depp, with long hair and chiseled features. A pang of recognition hits me, and I wonder where I might have seen him before.

"Hi," I say with another tiny wave.

"So, tell me, Eloise, what's bothering you?" she says, sliding her tiny body over the stools that separate us until she's right next to me. "Sweetie pie," she turns to the guy and motions for him to come over and bring the drinks. He does as she instructs. Turning to me again she asks, "What's he done?"

"Who?" I pretend as if she hasn't just figured me out in a matter of two minutes. She's more insightful than I initially thought.

"The guy who's got you exhaling like that. I'm an expert in this; I know when a girl is having boy trouble. I mean, I'm an interior designer by trade, but I could've been a couples' counselor. I just know it, right sweetie?" she says, turning to the guy and sweeping a strand of her blonde hair behind her ear.

"Yep," he agrees and throws back the remainder of his beer, then quickly asks for another.

"Oh, it's not like that." I wiggle in my seat like a nervous child, sip my wine, and avoid all eye contact with her.

"Yes it is," she says, turning her body toward me, urging me to speak.

We were the only ones sitting at the bar, and a

sudden urge came over me. I found myself thinking that maybe it wouldn't be the worst thing in the world to unburden myself. Perhaps talking about it could alleviate some of the tension that's been building up inside me, especially now. This stranger might just be the heaven-sent confidant I needed.

I swiveled on my stool, letting out a sigh of relief, and replied, "You're right." I had no idea I would feel so much better just by saying those words.

"I knew it," she exclaimed, a triumphant smile spreading across her face. "See sweetie, I'm never wrong about these things." She playfully elbows her boyfriend, hoping to capture his full attention. He obliges, turning toward her briefly, but then his eyes flick back to his phone.

"Okay, it's complicated," I confess, my words tumbling out in a rush.

I take a deep breath and plunge ahead. "I met a guy six months ago and when our connecting flights were cancelled, we spent a very intense twenty hours together."

"How intense?" she asks, resting her perfectly manicured hand on mine. Her eyes twinkle with intrigue, and I could feel the heat rising in my cheeks.

"Very, very intense," I admit, my voice barely above a whisper.

"What's got you exhaling like that?" She points at my mouth, and I bite my lip self-consciously. "I thought it was a one-time thing, that I would never see him again. But I just ran into him and I'm not even close to over him."

"Okay, does he know how you feel?"

"No. he doesn't. At least I don't think so."

"Aw, is that why you're sad?"

"No. And I'm not sad. I'm confused," I explain.

"Because it's complicated?" she asks, nodding in understanding.

"Yes."

"I'm not seeing the complication," she says.

That's because I'm not even mentioning Chris, Susie or my parents. And I'm not planning to.

"Just trust me. It's complicated."

"I recommend you forget all the complications and just be honest!"

"I wish it were that easy."

"Ugh, airlines, they're the worst," says the woman who was on the phone when I came in. She's with them. "White wine, please?" she tells the bartender.

"Eloise, this is our friend, Maria," says Ava, introducing us.

"Hi." Maria waves at me from a few stools down and takes a seat next to Ava's boyfriend.

"I'm gonna go," I say suddenly feeling like I've shared too much. I drop cash on the bar and stand.

She mirrors my stance and then puts her hands on my shoulders. "Tell him. If I know men, and I do, he probably already knows and is just waiting for you to say something."

It only takes a half second to see things clearly, like Ava,

"You're right," I say with a confident smile. Has this beautiful stranger really convinced me to go for it?

I'm now eager to get back to the cabin and make things right with Trevor. I want to apologize and start fresh, to move past the complications. Maybe we can even tell Susie, and maybe she'll understand why I lied about so many things.

"It was nice meeting you, all of you. Merry Christmas," I say.

"Oh, Merry Christmas, Eloise!" Says Ava, pulling me into an excited and warm hug. I return it with a smile, feeling grateful for her.

"Bye," I say one last time, before hurrying to my car. I want to get back to the cabin before I have a chance to talk myself out of what I'm about to do. It's time to take a chance, to be brave and vulnerable, and to see where this crazy journey takes me.

CHAPTER 15

Trevor

When Eloise storms away, I feel a pang of regret and frustration. I want to go after her, to make things right and clear the air. But I know that I've already made things bad enough, and I don't want to push her away even further.

I did everything tonight that I promised Susie I wouldn't do, and everything that Eloise didn't need. It's a sinking feeling, knowing that I've let them both down.

After I clean up, I grab a beer from the fridge, twist off the cap, and take a long swig. The cold, bitter liquid soothes my parched throat, but it can't dull the ache I feel.

I head to the living room, and I plop down on the couch, with the guilt heavy on my shoulders. I glance around the room, taking in the flickering embers of the dying fire. The room feels colder now, less welcoming than it was earlier.

As I take another sip of my beer, I'm suddenly transported back to that airport lounge again, where Eloise and I got to know each other better. It feels like a lifetime ago, and yet the memory is so vivid, so tangible.

I remember it started out rocky, but it didn't last.

"You have a nice face," I said, not really thinking about my choice of words.

Her reaction was exactly as I imagined it would be. "A nice face? That's a first," she said, laughing and taking a sip of her wine.

"What I mean is that you have a kind face," I explained, hoping to make amends.

Her expression softened at my words, and she smiled warmly. "That's better. And thank you. I've never heard that before," she said, her eyes meeting mine.

"Well, it's the truth," I insisted, feeling a sense of conviction in my words.

And I meant it. Sure, Eloise was undeniably beautiful, with her striking features and warm smile but what I was talking about went deeper than that. I could sense a kindness in her, a genuine concern for others that shone through.

Now that I know she's a doctor, it all makes sense. Her entire career is about caring for others, about putting their needs before her own. It's a noble calling, and one that requires a special kind of person.

"You have a kind face, Eloise," I repeated. "But it looks like you also carry a heavy burden. You can put it down. You don't have to carry it while you're with me. Forget about everything that's worrying you while we're in this space of waiting."

She looked at me with a mixture of confusion and curiosity, her eyes searching mine. "I don't know what you mean," she said, her voice hesitant.

"I think you do," I said gently, sensing her reluctance to open up. "You don't have to share it with me if you don't want to. I just want to offer you the chance to be someone who's not burdened, if only for a moment."

I didn't know what was bothering her, but I knew something was. Because although she had a kind face, her eyes were glazed with worry. She probably saw no point in denying what was so blatantly obvious to me because without another argument she finally met my eyes and nodded slightly.

"What about you? What burdens you? And, can you let it go too?" she asked, surprising me.

"I'm not burdened by anything," I admitted.

"Oh c'mon. Everyone's burdened by something.

Work? Money? A girl," she teased.

"A girl?"

"Yeah. You can't tell me you're just this happy go lucky guy all the time."

"I wouldn't put it that way, but I stopped worrying a while ago."

"And there it is," she said, pointing at me.

I suppose Eloise was on to something. It's kind of hard not to think about my accident and near-death experience whenever I'm in any serious conversation about life. But I wasn't sure if I wanted to tell her about it. I only talked about what I experienced when I found it necessary, when I thought it could help people understand me better or make a difference in their own lives. I wasn't some walking poster for death and resurrection, after all.

"Okay, fair enough. But it's not what you think."

"No, you're not running away from something?" Eloise asked me, her voice tinged with curiosity.

"Whoa, what makes you say that?" I asked, genuinely curious.

"I don't know," she said, her eyes searching mine. "People aren't usually as happy as you are."

I chuckled at that. "I'm not that happy," I said. "I just try to enjoy each moment as it comes."

But she wasn't convinced. "Come on," she said, exploding into a wide smile. "Look at you. You have a permanent grin on your face. And you're..." she paused, searching for the right word. "Light. That's the best way I can describe it."

"Light?" I repeated.

"Yes. "You said I could put my burden down. You only recognized that because you're walking around weightless, and it shows. You're bright. Like I said, light."

"Thank you. But the truth is, I don't worry because I appreciate life. And I don't want to waste a single minute of it with worry."

"Why?" She leaned forward, resting one hand on her face, while the other delicately circled the top of her wine glass.

I could sense that she wasn't going to let me get away with not answering her question. And deep down, I knew that I couldn't bring myself to lie to her. I hated liars, and I wasn't about to become one. I decided to tell her the truth, knowing that she deserved and perhaps even needed to hear it.

As I revealed the truth about my accident to Eloise, I could see the shock and concern etched on her face. She lowered her hand slowly from her face, and she stopped all fidgeting, looking at me with a mix of disbelief and sympathy.

"I'm so sorry. I didn't mean—" she began, but I interrupted her gently.

"Eloise, it's okay. I came back," I said, laughing a little at my own words as I always did, as if the reveal was a surprise to both of us.

Her eyes wandered around, as did the muscles in her face as she searched for the right words to say. I'd seen that look before on others, so I knew it well.

"I'm fine. It's behind me now. You ask why I'm happy, that's why. I learned that life is a gift that shouldn't be wasted."

Now, I find myself wavering between seeing Eloise tonight or not. I have to admit to myself that I'm not sorry for what happened between us. The kiss we shared was something I wanted, and still do. With that realization, I decide not to risk seeing her again. But just as I'm about to head upstairs, the door flings open and she is standing in the doorway.

CHAPTER 16

Eloise

As I walk through the front door, my heart is pounding with uncertainty. Will Trevor even want to hear me out after the way I left? I'm lost in my anxious thoughts when I see him standing at the bottom of the stairs.

"Hi," he says, looking a bit taken aback. Like I've caught him off guard.

"Hey. Can we talk?" I ask tentatively.

"Of course."

As he motions for us to head to the living room, I feel a flutter of anxiety in my chest. I wonder if he even wants to talk to me, or if he's just trying to be polite. But as we make our way to the living room, I hear him let out a small breath, almost like a sigh of relief. The sound sends shivers down my spine, and I feel a sense of comfort wash over me.

"Are you cold?" he asks, noticing my shiver. "I can start a fire if you want."

He seems to have misunderstood me. It was him, not the room that gave me shivers. "No, I'm okay," I reassure him.

I was about to explain myself and apologize for having left the way I did, but he beat me to it.

"I shouldn't have kissed you if you didn't want me to," he says, his words tentative and unsure. "Did you not want me to?" he asks, searching my eyes.

"It's complicated."

"Help me understand?" he offers, keeping his distance from me.

My heart pounds in my chest as he speaks, his words sending shockwaves through me. I want to tell him the truth, to confess everything about Chris and about lying to him. But the words catch in my throat, and I find myself unable to speak.

My mind races as I try to process everything. I want to tell him that his sister means everything to me, that I'm afraid of losing her if she ever finds out about what I did. But the fear of rejection and shame keeps me silent.

As I sit there, struggling to find the right words, I realize that I'm not ready for the confession. My emotions are a jumbled mess, and I feel like I'm drowning in them.

"Trevor, I'm sorry for—"

A sudden knock at the door interrupts our conversation, and we both turn to face it. I stay put, while he goes to answer it. As he leaves, I think about what I want to say. I want to assure him that he did nothing wrong, even though some part of me knows that what we did was wrong. But I also know that it can never happen again, even if it was amazing. That last part I would keep to myself.

There's a bit of excitement at the front door, so I approach to see the source of the commotion. I hear Trevor's voice greeting someone. But then I hear a familiar woman's voice, and my heart sinks. I know that voice. As I step into the foyer, I see Trevor hugging Ava.

"Oh no!" I blurt out unintentionally. All three of them turn to look at me.

"Hey, it's Eloise," says the guy, pointing at me with a mischievous smile that reminds me of Trevor's.

"Eloise, what are you doing here?" Ava comes rushing to me, embracing me in a hug.

"You all know each other?" Trevor asks perplexed.

"Not exactly," I say.

"We just met at the bar," Ava explains with a smile.

I try to keep my face neutral, hoping she won't reveal the secrets I shared earlier tonight. I feel like

I'm screaming inside my head, begging her not to give me away. My heart drops as I realize that her attentive boyfriend is Trevor's own brother. I want to disappear into thin air.

"Hey you," says Maria pushing back the door, just as Trevor was about to close it.

"Maria?" says Trevor, and his tone tells me he's not entirely thrilled with this surprise.

I like that he's not happy to have this beautiful woman here.

"Oh, we were all stuck at the airport as her flight was cancelled too. I told her no way she was spending Christmas in an airport," says, Ava, turning to them, but still at my side.

I notice Trevor's jaw clench. He's clearly uncomfortable, but he's trying his best to be a good host.

"Is it okay?" asks Maria, noticing Trevor's stiff demeanor.

I might not be the most perceptive person in this room, but I know tension. And there's definitely tension between those two.

"Of course, let me help you," says Trevor, taking her luggage and helping her out of her coat.

My attention is suddenly pulled away from Trevor and Maria by Ava's excited yet hushed squeal. "Oh my God, is Trevor the guy you were talking about?" she whispers.

My heart drops to my stomach, and I feel mortified. "Please, don't say anything. I haven't talked to him. I haven't said anything. I just can't," I plead, my anxiety skyrocketing.

"Hey sweetie," she says taking my hands in hers. "My lips are sealed." She slides her fingers across her lips.

"I'll make sure Chase knows to mums the word too. Your secret is safe with us."

"Thank you," I say because I believe she will. "But what about her? I ask, gesturing toward Maria.

"She doesn't know anything."

My breathing settles a bit now that I've got confirmation from Ava.

"Everyone's already in bed?" asks Chase.

"Yeah, it's been a long day, you know how it is. Let's get out of the cold." Trevor ushers them in, away from the foyer.

We're getting ready to go to the living room, when Laura cries out Chase's name. She's hurrying downstairs, with Mike, Dave and Susie following behind.

"I thought you weren't going to make it in today?" says Laura.

"Yeah. That was a lie. I wanted to surprise you."

They all exchange hugs, and as soon as they're finished Laura moves everyone into the living room.

"Mike, dear, can you start a fire, please?"

"On it." He grabs a few logs leftover from when Trevor brought them in and proceeds to get things started.

"Maria, how have you been? It's been, oh what four, five years?" Laura says, turning to look at Trevor for the answer.

"Five," both Trevor and Maria say in unison.

"Oh, that's right?" And your parents, how are they?"

Laura continues talking to Maria, but I've stopped paying attention now. My ears had perked up when Trevor and Maria had given their synchronized answer, but now my eyes are fixed on Trevor. What the hell was that about? He catches my eye and holds my gaze as if no one else is in the room. I should look away, but I don't want to. I want to read his expression and understand what's happened between him and Maria. It feels too long, like we shouldn't look at each other like this in front of everyone, but neither of us seems to care. I only tear my eyes away when I hear Susie say my name.

"Eloise, were you introduced to everyone yet?"

"We already met," says Ava, looping an arm around mine.

"Really?" How so?"

"Oh, we met about an hour or so ago, at Scrooge. Isn't that so, sweetie?" says Ava turning to me.

"I wanted to explore the town, so I borrowed your

van. I hope that's alright," I lie.

Susie's response is immediate and somewhat shocked. "Of course, Eloise!"

I'm relieved.

This weekend just got a whole lot more difficult. I'm starting to wonder if going home and facing Chris might've been easier.

"Honey, come here. Let Maria feel your belly," calls Laura.

For the first time since arriving here, I feel like a true stranger in the midst of the family catching up with each other. I should follow Susie and stand by my best friend to feel more comfortable, but instead I scan the room, looking for Trevor. He's not here. Before I do what I'm about to do, I examine the room. No one will notice if I step away, right? Right.

CHAPTER 17

Trevor

It's freezing outside but being in the chilly night air is preferable to being inside. As I exited, I made sure to grab my camera, thinking it could serve as a justification for my sudden departure. The Christmas lights outside are never switched off, so I'm not in complete darkness, but it wouldn't bother me if I were. The moon is particularly stunning tonight, its radiance casting a captivating glow over the festive town. I quickly took a photo, eager to capture the moment.

I look at the camera screen, hit menu and review the photo. Not the best, but a memory all the same.

"Hey, you okay?"

I don't have to turn to see who it is, but I do

anyway.

"Yeah, I'm fine. Just taking some photos." The truth, and not an excuse after all.

Eloise closes the door behind her but doesn't get very far from it. I half expect her to go back in, but when she doesn't, I'm glad. She comes down the few steps it takes to meet me and stands next to me.

"Can I see?" she asks, nodding towards my camera.

"Sure."

As I hold out the camera to Eloise, she steps closer to me, causing our arms to brush against each other. I don't know if she notices the way I do. She's making me absolutely crazy.

"It's beautiful the way you captured the town."

"Thanks," I say, and leave out that I was actually trying to capture the moon.

The memory of our kiss earlier resurfaces in my body now that the shock from Maria's appearance has faded. It's Eloise my mind is consumed by.

"So Maria, huh?" she says, surprising me.

"It's not what you think?"

"Oh, no? You weren't a thing?"

"No, we actually weren't."

"Oh," she says, surprised.

I don't know why Eloise is here with me, instead of inside with the rest of the family, but I like that she's here. What I don't like is that even with her coat on, she's shivering.

"Cold?" I ask.

"No, not really," she responds, teeth chattering.

"Here, I'll let you wear my coat, but you gotta promise to give it back," I tease, winking at her.

"No, I can't. You'll freeze," she protests.

"I'll be fine," I insist and wrap my coat around her. And once again we're in that familiar spot, where our eyes meet and no words are spoken. Her eyes seek my face and I follow her eyes until they land on my mouth.

"Better?" I ask.

She nods, and it's me that now traces the corners of her mouth with my eyes. I'm not making the same mistake twice in one night. I step back and think of ways to shut down anything else between Eloise and me.

"So Maria," I start. "She was my best friend for years. And it worked for us even though everyone told us that men and women couldn't be friends because inevitably one falls for the other. We didn't care what anyone said because we were 10 years strong."

"And what happened?" she asks, curiously.

"I died, came back and confessed my love to her."

She doesn't miss a beat, she dives right in, just as always.

"I see. And what happened then?"

"I wasn't what she wanted."

I blow out an exhausted breath and it surprises me. Maybe because it's the first time I've put it that way, and my ego is still a bit hurt. But that's it. Just my ego. I've had plenty of time to heal from that experience and although I lost Maria as my best friend, we remained civil. Which is why I assume she accepted Chase and Ava's invitation to come stay with us.

"I'm sorry to hear that."

"Nothing to be sorry about, really."

"So why are you out here then?"

"I haven't seen her in five years. Seeing her again brought back memories from that time. It wasn't always easy, back then. I mean with the recovery and decisions I had to make."

"Oh," she says.

I can see the war in her expression. Should she ask more? Should she stop? She must've heard enough because she doesn't continue. She just stares out at the sea of stars gathered in the sky. She looks beautiful, and peaceful, just the kind of energy I gravitate toward these days.

We stand in comfortable silence for a while. Having her here feels nice, like home and I can't explain it. I wouldn't dare say any of this to her. What would she think? I know exactly what she would think. That I'm absolutely crazy for feeling the way I do.

After we've exhausted our silence, she begins to talk.

"You should come back inside, I'm sure everyone's missing you." She says, taking off my coat and handing it back.

I don't agree or disagree, but I don't take my eyes off her as she leaves to go inside. Before she steps inside, she turns to me.

"You know that picture you took, of the town?"

"Yeah."

"The moon is my favorite part."

"Mine too."

Her eyes crinkle a little in the corners, it's barely a smile, but I take it. She goes inside without saying anything else. When the door closes, I take a few steps back away from the house and snap a photo before I go inside.

CHAPTER 18

Eloise

I sneak upstairs, so no one notices I've been out in the cold with Trevor. I guess sneaking around becomes a thing when I'm with him. As soon as I reach the top of the stairs, I make a beeline for the bathroom to remove my makeup then I saunter to my room. I usually sleep in an oversized t-shirt, but tonight's different. I've packed my comfiest and most festive pajamas for this trip, and I'm determined to wear each pair at least once. So tonight, it's the red pajamas adorned with little Santas all over. Even though they're long-sleeved and come with pants, the chilly air seeps through the walls, so I slipped on a long pair of cozy socks to keep my feet warm.

Now as I crawl under the covers it dawns on me

that I haven't checked my phone the entire time I've been here. It's as good a time as any to do so. I pick up my phone and as I scroll through the notifications, my heart sinks. I have five missed calls and five texts from Chris. To make matters worse, I also have three missed calls and two voicemails from my mom. I decided not to listen to the voicemail because I can't deal with whatever is on the other end of that. At least not tonight. Chris, I can deal with.

Chris: Peaches, call me when you get off.

Chris: Peaches?

Chris: Peaches New Years? You, me, New York? What do you think?

Chris: Call me as soon as you can, trying to book the tickets.

Chris: I booked it. I know you don't like me interfering but I'm going to call to get those days off for you. What's the point of being chief of staff if I can't get my girlfriend a few days off.

"No!"

That was yesterday.

Me: Hey sorry it's been crazy here. No. Don't do that! I'll ask for the days off myself.

The message is delivered and read. But there's no immediate response and my heart slips back and forth between my stomach to my chest. No three dots indicating he's responding.

Me: Chris?

Again, read. But no response. I wait a few minutes but still nothing. I can't sit and wait any longer. I muster the strength to call him. It rings once and then goes straight to voicemail.

I muster even more strength and listen to the voicemails my mom left.

"Eloise…. Eloise. Oh, great I got her voicemail."

"Eloise where are you? Chris is here and he's distraught over your behavior. The Sullivan's are also very disappointed. You're embarrassing your father. Call us this instant."

I turn off my phone, put it on the nightstand and turn the light off. Well, it's all out now. Part of me is relieved that it happened this way. The other part is backpedaling and dreading the apology I'm going to have to deliver.

As I lay my head on the pillow, I don't bother coming up with an apology tonight. Instead, I do what I haven't allowed myself to do since the night I snuck out of that hotel room. I think about Trevor without any reservations.

Six months ago, we crashed into my room kissing and grabbing at each other like we were about to burst. I hadn't felt this passionate for anyone in a long time and it was exhilarating. But before we got too far, I needed to freshen up.

"Shower," I managed to moan into his mouth.

"Okay," he breathed, putting me down after

releasing my legs which were wrapped around him.

I rushed to the bathroom, undressed, and jumped in the shower. I wasn't trying to have a relaxing shower, nor was I trying to talk myself out of what I wanted to happen. I just wanted to wash off the muck of having been on an airplane and then an airport for so many hours.

I hadn't bothered with shutting the bathroom door, and when he passed by, to wash his hands, he caught a glimpse of me through the glass door. He turned away, giving me privacy but I didn't want him to look away.

He finished washing his hands, and then turned to dry them and when he did, I pushed the shower door open. An invitation I wanted him to accept.

His eyes darted toward me and his gaze traveled slowly from my feet to my face, as if he was taking in every inch of me. It felt like a spotlight was shining on me, exposing me completely. When his eyes finally met mine, he raised an eyebrow in question, silently asking if I was sure about this. Without hesitation, I pushed the door open wider, inviting him in.

I resisted the urge to watch him strip off his clothes, and it wasn't until he was in the shower with me that I allowed myself to indulge in my desire to look at him. And he was a sight to behold. Every inch of his toned body was a work of art, from the chiseled abs to the intricate tattoos adorning his skin. I couldn't help but take it all in, my eyes tracing every curve and contour with a hunger that I couldn't quite suppress.

It was the moment we had been building up to, the culmination of all the tension and attraction that had been simmering between us all day. And when it finally happened, it was like a burst of fireworks, the explosion of pleasure and desire taking over.

Hours later, we found ourselves lost in each other once again. The intensity had subsided, replaced by a gentle and familiar rhythm as we explored each other with gentle touches and whispered words of affection.

As the night turned into morning, the heaviness of guilt settled into every crevice of my being. The need to escape became overwhelming, and I knew I had to leave. I carefully lifted his arm that was draped over my waist and dressed as quickly and quietly as possible. I was sure that this would be the last time I saw him.

Now, in this room, in his family's cabin, the decisions made that night weighs heavily on me once again. I throw the pillow over my head and scream into it, loud enough to let out some frustration, but not loud enough for anyone else to hear. As it turns out allowing myself to remember that night wasn't the best idea because it just reminded me of why I snuck out the way I did. Sure, I was feeling guilty over cheating on Chris—even though he had just cheated on me. But more than anything, the way Trevor made me feel in the mere twenty-four hours we spent together scared the hell out of me.

Ugh, enough. If I plan on waking up tomorrow at a decent time, I have got to put all these thoughts away. No more Trevor. Or Chris. Or my parents.

As I lay in bed, I find myself counting sheep like a child, hoping to drift off into a peaceful sleep. The gentle rhythm of my breath and the soft sounds of the night outside my window add to the soothing ambiance. Just as I begin to feel my body relax and surrender to sleep, a single thought slips into my mind like a thief in the night. It's an exciting one, though: I can't wait to see Trevor in the morning.

CHAPTER 19

Trevor

As soon as I stepped back inside the house, I realized that the family was still catching up. Despite feeling exhausted, I knew I couldn't go to bed just yet. It would have appeared as though I was intentionally avoiding Maria, or worse, that I cared that she was here.

Maria and I have known each other since high school, and she had been a constant part of my life for a decade. Naturally, she became a part of my parents' lives as well. They all know what transpired between us, and I sense that my parents have been secretly hoping for Maria to change her mind, even though it's been five years. Sometimes, it feels as though they were more affected by the rejection than

One Christmas With You

I was.

"There you are," says Mom the moment she spots me.

I scan the room for Eloise but she's not there.

"Did you take any good pics?" asks Susie noticing the camera in my hand.

"I think so."

"Nice," she says.

"Come sit," says Mom, patting the spot between her and Maria.

I sit between them, and honestly, it's the most uncomfortable I've been.

I'm half checked out as the conversations dance between the town's Christmas decorations and the bad weather they experienced on the way. But now, I'm all in as they discuss sleeping arrangements.

"Maria dear, the guest room is taken by Susie's friend Eloise. The only other bed we have is in Trevor's room, which is a very comfortable pullout. You don't mind sharing your room, do you sweetheart?" says Mom turning to me.

"Not at all," I say.

Maria hesitates before responding. "Are you sure it's okay? I don't want to impose."

I can feel the tension in the air as everyone waits for my response. The anticipation is palpable.

"It's perfectly fine," I say with a reassuring smile, trying to ease Maria's concern. After all, I really don't care.

But if my mom is trying to play matchmaker, she's way off the mark.

"Oh good! C'mon, let me get you settled in," says Mom.

"Yes, I'm exhausted," says Ava.

Mom, Maria and Ava all stand and start to go upstairs.

"You coming?" says Ava to Chase.

"Be right there, need a minute with my bro."

"That's my cue," says Susie, "Be good you two knuckle heads."

"Night Sus," I tell her.

Chase's body language is practically shouting out his eagerness to speak with me. I can't fathom what it could possibly be about, but it's clear that whatever it is, is making him nervous. Being the middle child, I've grown accustomed to reading my siblings like a book. With Susie, I can tell that she's feeling an inexplicable sense of pity toward me, despite there being no reason for it. Every time she glanced my way, she tilted her head sympathetically, silently communicating she feels bad for me.

But there's no reason for it. I harbor no yearning for Maria, nor do I desire anything from her. I don't indulge in any nostalgia or entertain the thought of what could have been. I hold the unwavering belief that everything unfolded exactly as it was meant to.

Chase, on the other hand, has a nervous habit of bouncing his leg and biting his nails whenever he's hiding something or keeping a secret. It's a telltale sign that he's up to something. As soon as I sat down, I noticed his leg bouncing and the sound of his teeth clicking against his nails. He's never been good at keeping secrets, and I can tell he's holding something back.

"What's going on Chase, you alright?"

"Oh yeah." He moves from one nail to another, until Susie's completely out of sight.

"Bro, I'm doing it," he spills, excitedly.

"Doing what?"

He sticks his hand in his pocket and pulls out a small box.

"Proposing to Ava," he confesses.

At first, I remain silent, trying to process the unexpected news. As I take a closer look at Chase's face, I can tell he's not kidding around. My mind is still reeling from the shock as I reach for the box he's holding out to me. Slowly, I open it.

"Wow!"

Chase nods eagerly, his leg bouncing with excitement as he speaks. "Yeah, and I'm also moving back home to run the business with Dad," he adds.

I'm still in disbelief as I try to wrap my head around the fact that my 25-year-old brother is getting married and settling down.

"Dad knows?" I finally managed to ask.

Chase grins broadly, "Yeah, I called him a while back and told him about the proposal and coming back home, the whole thing. He's stoked," he replies.

"Congrats, man," I say, standing and giving him a tight hug. I feel a surge of pride for my little brother.

I'm happy he's found someone who makes him truly happy. Plus, he's fulfilling Dad's dream of having one of his sons run the business with him.

"How about you, bro?" he asks.

"What about me?" I reply.

"Dad mentioned you were leaving?"

"Just for a little while."

"Really?" he asks.

He seems surprised.

"Yeah, why?" I ask, sensing something unspoken.

"I don't know. I just thought maybe...ah, never mind," he trails off.

"That I was ready to move back home too?" I suggest.

"Kinda. Dad loves you, you know?" he admits.

"I know," I say, with assurance. Love is not the problem here.

"What about Eloise?" Chase asks, sliding the ring back into his pocket.

"Eloise?" I repeat, my eyebrows furrowing in confusion.

"Yeah, man. That girl's into you," he says with a

smirk.

I roll my eyes.

"You're crazy. Let's just go to bed," I say, shoving him.

"I'm telling you, she is, bro. You're so blind," he says, playfully punching my arm.

"Sure, I am," I say, shaking my head and heading towards my room. Chase follows me, still talking about Eloise, but I tune him out.

As I make my way to my room, I steal a glance at Eloise's closed door. I wonder if she's already asleep. My mind races with the possibility of what could happen if I went to her, but I quickly shake the idea away and remind myself that it's not the right thing to do. With a deep sigh, I grip the doorknob of my own room and reluctantly step inside.

CHAPTER 20

Eloise

Christmas eve

I woke up early to make sure I could get ready before the morning rush. As I finish up, I can hear the sounds of laughter, chatter, and even singing downstairs. I'm thrilled that Christmas music is playing this early, making for a perfect start to Christmas Eve.

I decided on a green sweater adorned with a snowman, inspired by the ornament I received yesterday, paired with jeans and matching boots. Before heading downstairs, I apply a bit of lip gloss to complete the look.

I step out of my bedroom, giddy as a child chasing a butterfly, eager to join the festive mood downstairs. My mind is so preoccupied with the anticipation of what awaits me that I barely notice my surroundings. Suddenly, Maria's voice jolts me out of my thoughts. She's standing in front of me in a robe, coming out of Trevor's room, when she greets me. "Good morning! Anyone in the bathroom?"

I shake my head. I'm stunned speechless but then I catch myself, "Morning. No. All free."

"Thanks," she says, floating past me.

Eloise get it together. This is none of your business.

I get moving again, but the light and airy pep I had has vanished. I hit the foyer, and now I can really hear the music. It's coming from the living room. But it sounds like everyone's in the kitchen. I need a minute alone to calm down, so I turn to the living room and hope that I'm right and no one's there, but I don't get very far.

"Eloise, we're in here," says Susie waving me toward the kitchen but coming into the foyer. "I need my phone, showing Mom the breast pump, I saved," she says reaching into her purse and grabbing her phone.

"Oh, okay," I say and follow her.

"Look who's up," she says as if they've been waiting for me.

"Morning, darling," says Laura.

"Morning," I say to her and everyone else.

Mike, Dave and Grandpa Carl are at the table but there's no Trevor. Maybe he's still upstairs in the room.

"Come sit," says Susie pointing to the stool next to her.

I do, and she immediately starts sharing photos with Laura. I should leave them alone or join them in the conversation, but I'm consumed with curiosity. I have to know where Trevor is.

"Where's everyone else?" I ask trying to be casual about it.

"Ava and Chase went into town. Ava wanted to go into some retro store she saw last night to get something she swore wouldn't be there if she waited any longer. Trev and Maria are sleeping, I guess."

"Well maybe those two worked it out," says Laura.

I don't have to ask who she's talking about, but I do anyway.

"Who?"

"Oh Mom, you have to give that up," says Susie. "She's talking about Maria and Trev. Once upon a time he had a thing for her, but he's over it, I can tell. Mom needs to stop, right, Mom?"

"Oh I just want Trevor to be happy."

"I am happy."

The moment I hear him, my heart leaps a million times over.

As I turn to face him, he's leaning against the

doorframe, wearing a wide grin that immediately irks me. I quickly avert my gaze, hoping he doesn't notice. But before I know it, he's placing a hand on my lower back as he saunters past me.

"Eloise," he says.

I stiffen at his touch, but I don't offer a good morning.

I glance up and catch sight of what else he's wearing besides that infectious smile of his. He has on a pair of fitted jeans and a black long-sleeved shirt that hugs his forearms. I notice his tattoos peeking through, and I'm entranced by them as usual. Quickly, I avert my gaze before he catches me staring. He grabs a piece of bacon from a plate on the counter and pours himself a cup of coffee.

"Wait for the rest," Laura gently reprimands.

"Coffee?" he says to me.

"Sure," I say, staring at him as if he's just stolen my cookie.

"Black, right?" he says, already pouring it.

"Yes."

"How do you know that?" asks Susie, surprised.

We both stare at her for what feels like forever, but then it occurs to me that neither of us are saying anything.

"I told him on our trip into town. Had a few cups. It was cold."

"Oh, that's right. Pregnancy brain," she says,

getting back to her phone.

The truth is, he learned this little fact about me the first hour we spent together on that plane.

Trevor and I exchange a "that was close" look, but when he offers me a smile, I don't return it. He cocks his head, looking confused, and I savor the feeling of satisfaction that I've caught him off guard.

I have no reason, not a single one to be upset over what I just witnessed, and yet I'm burning with jealousy.

"Morning everyone," says Maria.

It takes everything in me to not roll my eyes. I don't say good morning, because I've already said it once to her, instead I offer the smile I didn't give Trevor.

"Coffee?" asks Trevor.

"Yes please, thank you."

He pours her a cup, adds cream and sugar and hands it to her. I guess he's a barista this morning, preparing coffee just like everyone likes it. My feelings of annoyance continue.

"How did you sleep, Maria?" asks Laura.

I don't want to stay and hear her answer. I just don't.

"I'll be right back," I interject before Maria can respond. All eyes turn to me. "I need to return a call to my parents."

"Is everything okay?" asks Susie.

"Yeah, they left a message last night, and I didn't get it till late. I just remembered. And you know how they are."

"I do. Better get to it," she says.

She doesn't ask for more information or mention Chris., and I'm glad. I make a swift escape and head straight upstairs. I'm about to enter my room when I hear my name.

"Eloise," says Trevor. "What's going on?"

"I should ask you the same thing," I say, trying my hardest to mask the jealousy in my voice.

What am I doing?

Trevor raises an eyebrow, catching on to my tone. "What's that supposed to mean?" he asks, a smirk forming on his face.

"You know what? Never mind," I say, turning to go inside my room, horrified.

"Hey," he says, putting a hand up, preventing the door from shutting and coming inside. "I have no idea why you're upset with me."

"That makes two of us."

"Okay. Wanna talk about it?"

I don't have it in me to lie about what's bothering me. So, I come right out with it.

"I saw Maria coming out of your room."

"So?"

"So I thought you didn't have feelings for her anymore?"

"Eloise. Eloise," he says playfully. "Are you jealous?"

"Oh God!" I roll my eyes, groan, and throw my hands over my face, throwing myself back on the bed.

"No, no, no. Come here," he says, grabbing both my hands and lifting me off the bed.

Our bodies are flush against each other, me looking up at him, and him staring at me with that wicked smile and those hazel eyes. That smile that seems to be only for me.

"I'm flattered," he says.

"I have no right."

"True. But I like it."

He's the absolute worst. But I like it.

"There's nothing between Maria and me. I told you the truth. She's just bunking in the only room that has an extra bed. Unless you want to switch with her?" he winks, and I can't be alone in this room for one more second with him.

"I need to get back downstairs," I tell him.

"That's what I thought," he says with a smirk, releasing my hands.

"I'm going," I say, and hurry to the door before we have a chance to make another mistake.

I leave my room and head downstairs, this time a little happier than on the way up.

CHAPTER 21

Trevor

I can't immediately go after Eloise because my body is still in a state of excitement. I stand there, feeling the heat rising in me, as I try to calm down. This woman has a hold on me that I can't seem to shake, and it's both thrilling and frustrating.

As I crawled into bed last night, Maria was already half asleep. We exchanged a simple "goodnight" and that was it. I was truthful when I said Maria was just staying in my room because it was the only one with an extra bed. I was also feeling hopeful when I offered Eloise the chance to switch rooms with her, even though I knew it was unlikely she would. Still, it was amusing to see Eloise's reaction to my suggestion. I couldn't deny the thrill I felt at the thought of sharing a room with her, even if it was just wishful thinking.

After all this time, one thing has become clear to me about Eloise — she doesn't seem to know what she wants. Her behavior is so inconsistent that I feel like I'm on a rollercoaster ride with her. And it makes me wonder if there's more going on, something she's not ready to share with me.

The first time we met, I gave Eloise all the space she needed. I didn't ask questions or dig into her personal life. I wanted her to share as much or as little as she wanted. Later I regretted that because when she left, I knew very little about her. I never thought that I would even want to find her, but as it turns out I did, and then I couldn't. But now, now that she's here, I feel like I'm getting a second chance but she's fighting it. Why? It can't be just Susie.

I'm good to go now, and so I make it back to the kitchen just as breakfast is being served. We take our seats and I'm disappointed that Eloise is not sitting next to me. Instead, she takes the seat across from me and next to Susie because Maria has taken that seat. I don't blame either of them. Even though Maria came with Chase and Ava, it's me who she knows best.

We're passing the food around, and clanking plates when Chase asks me something I know will sour Dad's mood.

"So what's your first stop?" asks Chase, referring to my trip.

"I arrive in Switzerland on New Year's Eve," I tell him, then ask him to pass the eggs.

"Nice." He scoops a spoonful of eggs on his plate and passes it down from Ava to Maria to me.

"You're going to Europe?" asks Maria.

"I am." I pass down the eggs to Mom, and grab one pancake, and some bacon.

"Why are you going there? I didn't know you ever wanted to go?"

"Let's just say I met someone who inspired me." I wink at Eloise not caring who sees.

She squirms in her seat, and her eyes travel to everyone in the room. I smile because seeing her squirm is cute, not to mention I'm hoping it pushes her over the edge and gets her to be truthful with me. I want to know what's holding her back. If it's me, then fine. But given recent events, I can confidently say I'm not the problem.

The only person that notices is Grandpa. Susie is busy talking to Dave. Dad is busy pretending not to listen, and Mom is going back and forth bringing extra napkins, salt, and pepper and whatever else she finds we're missing.

"Must be one special girl," says Maria.

This catches my attention. There's something in her tone that feels out of place. I glance at her, and she's staring at me, waiting for a response. My eyes narrow, and I cock my head unsure of what the hell she's doing. I'll bite.

"She is."

"Are you seeing someone? Is she going with you?" asks Susie.

"Let the boy eat," says Grandpa.

"Oh, it's okay Grandpa," I say.

"Not seeing her yet. But maybe things will change," I say, my eyes landing on Eloise once again.

Maria lets out a sound, only I can hear because of our proximity. I don't back down from whatever she's starting. I doubled down and looked at her to see if her sound revealed anything. As it turns out, it does. She glances between me and Eloise and back to her plate. She's on to us and I don't care.

"Let me take a photo," I say, standing and reaching for my camera.

I put the camera on a nearby shelf, set the timer and returned to the table. Only, I don't return to my seat.

"Everyone, look at the camera, ten-second timer." I hurry and stand between Eloise and Susie, placing one arm over Eloise.

One photo to mark the moment I confirmed I truly was over Maria.

CHAPTER 22

Eloise

I can feel the tension rising as Maria's eyes bore into me and Trevor. It's as if she can see right through us. Meanwhile, Susie is completely engrossed in her conversation with Dave and unaware of the brewing drama. I'm not too worried about Maria knowing, but her disapproval is palpable. It's clear that she doesn't like whatever is going on between Trevor and me.

I feel like I'm playing a game of hide and seek with Trevor, and I'm determined to win. The last thing I need is for him to blurt out our secret to Susie. So after breakfast, I stick to Susie's side like glue, chatting about the baby and the upcoming holidays, hoping to distract Trevor if he comes near. I know I'll have to tell Susie eventually, but right now I just want her to enjoy her pregnancy without any added stress. The thought of telling her that I was with her brother while I was with Chris makes my stomach turn. But I'll do it when the time is right. For now, I'll keep my guard up and hope Trevor keeps his promise not to reveal the truth.

After breakfast, we all gather outside, the chilly winter air nipping at our noses. The ground is blanketed with a fresh layer of snow, perfect for our snowman showdown. Susie, Ava, Maria and I are huddled together, waiting for Laura to arrive with the hat filled with names. My understanding is that after we build our snowman, we'll vote for our favorite creation, excluding our own. It's a fun cherished tradition that I'm grateful to be part of.

Standing together, I keep a low profile, not wanting to draw attention to myself or risk revealing anything. Maria's never-ending curiosity about Trevor has resurfaced once again though, and she turns to Susie for answers.

"So, who's the girl Trevor's seeing?" she asks.

Susie, ever the protective sister, responds with a hint of annoyance. "I don't know. Why do you care? I thought you weren't interested?"

My mouth drops open at the way Susie responds, but she's nothing if not blunt.

Maria shrugs, but I can see the interest in her eyes

"A girl's entitled to change her mind," she says, directing her response to me.

Before I have a chance to answer Ava interjects.

"Stop it, Maria," Ava chimes in, interlocking her arm with Maria's. "It's so cold out here," she says, shivering and leaning into Maria for warmth.

Susie shoots me a quick glance and rolls her eyes, clearly not caring if Maria notices her disapproval. I don't know why it makes me happy that she doesn't approve of Maria, but it does.

I spy Laura emerging from the house, and my curiosity is piqued. I can tell she has her sights set on Trevor. And sure enough, she makes a beeline for him, armed with a stylish grey scarf. He puts up a half-hearted fight, but she's not taking no for an answer. After a bit of back and forth, he gives in, begrudgingly slipping on the scarf. I have to admit, it suits him.

I find myself momentarily lost in thought, gazing at him with a glazed expression. But I quickly snap out of it and turn away, not wanting anyone, especially him, to catch me staring.

"Alright, I have the names right here," sings Laura, demanding our attention.

"About time," says Grandpa Carl.

"Grandpa?" says Susie.

Chase and Trevor laugh and come closer to where we're standing.

Thankfully, he's busy talking to Chase and is not drawing attention to us, unlike his behavior at breakfast.

"Honey, come here," says Laura, calling to Mike.

Dave sneaks up behind Susie, encircling his arms around her belly. She responds by placing her hands over his, and it's almost too sweet for words. It warms my heart to see them like this. As I watch them, a smile spreads across my face, and Susie notices and returns it with a kind smile of her own.

"Who wants to go first?" asks Laura.

"I'll go," says Maria.

"Alright, step forward."

Maria steps forward, and I can't help but judge her outfit. Her tight red shirt and black leather leggings cling to her athletic body, but it doesn't exactly scream Christmas. Her boots may not be snow boots, but they're high enough to keep her knees warm. Trevor's eyes linger on her, and a twinge of jealousy stirs within me again. I run my fingers through my hair in frustration before jamming my hands into my coat pockets, desperate for some semblance of warmth. But the carrot I had stashed in there after breakfast remains stubbornly cold, providing no relief from the biting winter air. Meanwhile, Maria seems impervious to the cold, sauntering around with her coat open, exposing herself and her figure-hugging outfit to the elements.

Laura calls for a drum roll, and Dave and Susie oblige. Their antics cause everyone to laugh, including me. Maria draws a name from the hat and announces who she's picked out. Unsurprisingly, it's Trevor's name that she's drawn. A wave of displeasure rises within me, but I try to brush it off and focus on the event. Susie looks at me and rolls her eyes, mouthing "of course." I smile at her response. As I glance over at Trevor, I see him high-fiving Maria, seemingly unfazed by the situation. Despite my annoyance, I'm determined to enjoy the Christmas Eve festivities and not let my emotions get in the way.

The drawing continues with Susie selecting Ava as her partner. Mike picks Chase, and Laura chooses Dave. That leaves me with Grandpa Carl as my partner for the snowman competition.

"We're going to crush this competition, kid," Grandpa Carl declares as he comes to stand next to me.

"You bet we are," I reply with a confident grin.

Laura sets the timer for one hour and announces the start of the competition. Without hesitation, everyone scatters in different directions, eagerly seeking out the perfect spot to build their snowy masterpiece. I, on the other hand, stay back with Grandpa Carl, matching his unhurried pace as we make our way across the snowy terrain. Although he's not exactly racing towards our designated area, I find myself enjoying the slower pace, allowing us the opportunity to discuss the type of snowman we want to create.

I turn to Grandpa Carl and ask, "So any ideas? You've done this before. Any clues as to what the winners usually look like?"

He responds, "It must be solid. The tighter we pack it, the stronger it can be, which means we can make a big one."

I nod in agreement, taking mental notes of his advice.

"I'll be honest, when Susie first told me we were doing this, I was a bit confused," I admit.

"Why's that?" Grandpa Carl asks.

"Don't all snowmen look the same?" I ask him with a chuckle.

"You'd think." He points to an open spot, and we steer our steps toward it.

We're between two teams, Susie and Ava and Trevor and Maria. In one way it's a blessing and in another it's a curse.

"But you have to remember," he continues. "It's about the integrity of the snowman."

"Integrity?" I repeat, not sure how that applies to building a snowman.

"Yep," Grandpa Carl affirms. "It must be strong from the start. If not, it will crumble." He bends down, grabs a hand full of snow and turns it until it's a neatly packed ball.

"See, solid. Integrity. With this type of attention to detail, we can build a winning snowman. We don't need scarves, and the perfect carrot. Those are just extras. Our snowman will stand for days. You understand?"

"Strong from the start?" I repeat and when I do, he arches an eyebrow and nods.

One look at him and I know what he's saying. I'm keenly aware that he knows about me and Trevor and he's not just talking about the snowman.

"It's not what you think?"

"It's none of my business. Just wanted to give you food for thought. Now let's get to building this snowman."

This family is my absolute favorite. Honesty and bluntness are so rare these days, but I truly embrace it. As a doctor, I must be blunt. I can't beat around the bush, and I don't. This way of communicating doesn't translate into my personal life, however badly I wish it did.

It's a blue cloudless wintery day, and this will go down as one of my favorite Christmas Eve activities. Grandpa Carl doesn't talk much, except when he's telling me to gather more snow, or pack it tighter. We're each gathering and building a large ball meticulously, in silence.

I stole a few glances over at Trevor and Maria and the last time I looked over, they were throwing snowballs at each other, and a shapeless snowman was starting to take form. I was annoyed by their playful banter but happy their snowman had no integrity. From where I stood, the temptation to keep looking over was too great so I changed positions. Now my back was to them.

As Grandpa Carl and I work on the bottom half of our snowman, Susie lets out a sudden yelp. Concerned, I quickly rushed over to her. "Are you okay?" I ask.

I'm not the only one who comes and runs over to her. "Hey what's going on?" asks Trevor.

He must have heard her even though he was farther away. Grandpa is now here too.

"I think it's a Braxton hick's," she says, holding her belly.

"You're 38 weeks, right?" I confirm.

"Yes."

"Okay. It's your body preparing you for labor. I'm sure everything's fine. Let's just keep an eye out, okay?" I tell her.

"Could you deliver this baby if you had to?" asks Susie. For the first time, I saw a hint of fear in her eyes.

"Of course I could. But it won't come to that."

"There's not a hospital in town. It will take at least thirty minutes to get to the closest hospital," she reminds me.

I reassure her. "Hey, don't worry. I'm here for you. You know that."

"I know. I think I'm going to have to sit the rest of the competition out. Sorry Ava," she says apologetically.

"It's okay," Ava responds, dragging out the word "okay." "I can't believe I might witness the birth of a baby."

"Let's not get ahead of ourselves. It's likely Braxton Hicks," I say, hoping to ease Susie's nerves.

"C'mon, we'll grab a couple of chairs and watch from over there," Grandpa Carl suggests, leading Susie toward the cabin and a spot where they can watch the rest of the competition.

"Sorry, kid. Looks like you'll need to find a new partner. Remember what I taught you," Grandpa Carl tells me as he and Susie head towards the cabin, Dave meets them halfway.

"What's going on?" asks Maria, as she approaches us.

"She might be in labor," Ava excitedly chimes in.

"She's not in labor," I clarify.

"At least we have a doctor in the house," says Trevor.

"That's why she asked if you could deliver the baby?" Ava finally catches on.

"I gotta get back to my snowman," I say, making

my way back.

"What do they call you, Dr. Eloise?" Ava calls after me. She's sweet but such a child.

"Dr. Parker," I yell back.

"Need some help?" Trevor offers. I turn to face them and observe their different expressions. Ava seems thrilled that Trevor is offering to help, while Maria's expression has softened, almost sad. I remember Grandpa Carl's advice about integrity and realize I might need some assistance if we want our snowman to stand a chance. "I do," I reply, waiting for Trevor to join me.

CHAPTER 23

Trevor

When Maria draws my name from the hat, I feel a twinge of disappointment. I was really hoping to be paired up with Eloise. I would've loved some time alone with her, but it seems like fate has other plans for us. On top of that, I can't shake the feeling that Maria has something up her sleeve, and it's making me uneasy.

We're all paired up now, and I'm thrilled to see that Eloise and Grandpa Carl are a team. I know they have what it takes to win, and seeing Eloise celebrate a win would make my day. Once Mom gives us the go-ahead, we all scatter to find our perfect snowman-building spot. I'm not in the mood to talk to Maria, and she seems to sense it.

"Cat got your tongue?" she says.

After debating for only a few seconds, I decided to be honest and confront her about what's been bothering me. "What was that back there?" I ask her, making my unease known.

"What?" she feigns ignorance.

"You know what."

"Can't a girl be curious?"

"Is that what that was?" I question, growing more frustrated.

I find a spot to build the snowman and come to a halt. It's at a distance from the others so that they can't hear our conversation.

I kneeled and started gathering the snow in a pile, waiting for Maria to answer. She bends down, ready to help. "Okay fine. You've got me," she admits. "How long have you known her?"

"Who?" I reply, feeling out how much she actually picked up on.

"Eloise?" she clarifies.

"Wow," I sigh in response.

Now that it's out in the open, I want her to stay out of it. I don't want to compromise Eloise and Susie's relationship. Given Maria's attitude at breakfast I can't say she'll be discreet about it.

"Why so touchy?"

I stand because this conversation deserves my full attention.

"Why do you care? You were very clear five years ago that I wasn't what you wanted. So, what is this?"

She stays quiet, with a distant expression. Perhaps she's trying to recall what she said to me five years ago.

"You're right. But I've done a lot of growing up and a lot of thinking. Truth is, you've been on my mind lately, and running into Chase felt like a sign. Then, seeing you again confirmed what I'd been feeling. I was wrong. I should've never let you go.

"You don't get to do that now. Not after five years. Not after I've moved on with my life."

"I know, I was just hoping..."

She doesn't continue because Grandpa and Eloise walk up and are a bit closer than the others are. I don't think they can hear so I go on.

"Look, I loved you for a long time. And I care about you still, as a friend."

She looks over my shoulder and I follow her eyes. Eloise is not paying attention to us, she's focused on Grandpa, so now she continues.

"I was just hoping it wasn't too late."

I must admit that I have been preparing for this moment for a while now. Even in the early days, I knew it was a possibility. But now that it's actually happening, I find myself wishing it wasn't. I don't want to entertain the thought of what could be. Not for a moment.

"I'll always be here for you. As the friend I started out as. Is that enough?" I ask her, fully aware that her answer won't change anything.

She bites her lip, considering my offer. I don't say it aloud, but I know that it's either friendship or nothing. I won't go backward, it's just not me.

"It will have to be," Maria finally concedes.

I nod, feeling relieved that we've had this conversation. It's like an important chapter of my life has finally closed. "Now let's finish this snowman," I say, moving on.

As Maria and I work together, it becomes apparent that our snowman is far from a winner.

"This sucks," Maria exclaims, throwing a snowball my way. I retaliate with a handful of snow, laughing and hoping this eases the tension between us. Soon after that exchange, our light-hearted moment is interrupted by a loud yelp from Susie.

***

I got my wish after all, a moment alone with Eloise, though I wish it had been under different circumstances.

"Thanks for helping," says Eloise, walking back to the snowman she started with Grandpa.

"My pleasure."

"Did you have fun building yours?" she says, glancing over at the snowman I made with Maria.

I've definitely done better in prior years, but with all the distractions, it was hard to focus. "It was okay," I say, shrugging my shoulders.

"Hmm," she says, piquing my curiosity.

"What's that?" I say as we reach her snowman.

The bottom half is already finished, so she starts a new ball for the top. I join her.

"It just looked like you were having a lot of fun."

I shake my head, feeling confused by her mixed signals.

"Can I ask you something and you be completely honest with me?" I ask.

"Sure," she replies.

"What's going on with you? What's the real reason you don't want Susie to know about us?"

She avoids my gaze and focuses on the snowball we're building, but it starts to fall apart, so she grabs more snow to compensate.

"I already told you the reason. I don't think she would understand," she replies, still not looking at me directly.

I sense that she's not being completely truthful, and it disappoints me. Honesty is important to me and without it, I don't see a path forward. Perhaps that's what she wants anyway.

"Are you sure that's all?" I give her another

chance to come clean.

"I'm sure," she says, doubling down on her lie.

"Okay. Let's finish this puppy. Looks like everyone else is already done.

We get into a steady rhythm of packing our snowman tightly until it feels solid. It's about three feet tall, with three imperfectly round sections. Once we know it's strong enough, we search the nearby grounds to find sticks for arms, and rocks for eyes. I took off the scarf Mom wrapped around my neck earlier and placed it around the snowman. Eloise reaches into her pocket and brings out a large carrot she said she'd been carrying around since breakfast.

"Pretty good," she says, stepping back to get a good look.

"It's perfect," I say.

A proud smile tugs at her lips. I regard her silently wanting to know her so much more than she's allowing me to. But I don't dare to say so and thankfully she doesn't notice my staring. She looks back and sees the family gathered around Susie and Grandpa Carl, each already finished with their snowman.

"Yeah, it's really good," she says turning back to the snowman.

"Ready?" I ask.

"Yeah, let's go."

CHAPTER 24

Eloise

The moment has arrived to choose the best snowman of the day, and my pick is already made. It belongs to Chase and Laura, whose creation is smaller than ours, with only two sections instead of three, but it's magnificent. Their snowman has two perfectly round rocks for eyes and a short, crooked carrot nose. I can tell Grandpa gave them the same advice he gave me. Their snowman is not only sturdy but playful, and I just love it.

"Alright, put the names in the hat," says Laura, taking the hat around to each of us. We all drop our folded-up slips of paper into the hat, and when we're finished, she stands in the middle of the circle, ready to deliver the results.

"Eloise and Trevor, 1 for you," she says to me.

But where is Trevor? He's been quiet since our conversation, and I wonder if he's upset with me. As someone who values honesty above all else, he must have sensed that something wasn't quite right.

"Chase and Laura, 1 for us," she says to Chase with a high five.

As she continues to call out names from the hat, we're all on the edge of our seats, waiting for the last name to be called. The snowmen all seem to be holding their breath too, with their coal eyes and carrot noses pointed towards Laura.

"This is it y'all," she says, her voice filled with excitement and anticipation. We all hold our breaths as she pulls out the final name. "Eloise and Trevor. Congratulations!" she announces, and I can feel my heart racing with excitement.

"Thank you, but it was Grandpa Carl that I owe this honor to," I say, half joking, half serious.

"I knew you could do it," he says, still sitting next to Susie.

"Thanks for your faith in me," I say with a smile.

"Congratulations bestie," says Susie, with a high five.

"Thanks. How are you doing?"

"I think I'm okay. They're coming every 30 minutes or so, but not getting any stronger."

"Okay. Good."

"Alright, let's get inside for some lunch," says Laura.

Everyone follows her lead, except for Trevor. I notice he's got his camera now, so I stop to see what he's doing. He turns toward the five snowmen and snaps a photo from a distance. I should go inside, but I linger a bit hoping he catches up to me, and he does.

"Just one?" I say, referring to his method of just taking one photo.

"One is all I need."

We're the last ones in, but I can hear that everyone's in separate rooms. Trevor heads to the kitchen, and I follow him. I'm in desperate need of hot chocolate. My hands are practically numb.

"Hey guys, congratulations again," says Ava.

"Yeah, you won fair and square. That was a solid snowman," says Chase.

He's sitting next to Ava, at the island, sipping on something warm.

"Thanks, but I didn't do much, it was all Eloise," says Trevor.

His tone is distant, like he's upset about something.

"Thank you, guys, I had a lot of fun," I say, trying to make up for his sour mood.

Trevor goes toward the coffee maker, and once again I follow because I'm grabbing a mug for my hot cocoa.

Ava's giddy over something.

"Uh-oh," she sings.

I turn to face her. I'm not following what she's doing.

"Look up," she says.

Trevor and I look up.

"It's a mistletoe. You know what that means," she says, rubbing her hands together.

"Ah, mistletoe," says Laura coming into the kitchen. "Ava, did you do that?" she asks, wrapping her arms around her. "I love your Christmas spirit."

"Nope. I don't think so," says Susie the moment she steps in the kitchen and notices Trevor and I under the mistletoe.

"Oh, stop it Susie, it's all in the Christmas spirit," says Laura.

"Kiss. Kiss. Kiss," Ava starts to chant.

"Kiss. Kiss. Kiss," says Chase. Then Laura, followed by Mike, Dave. Everyone but Susie.

I look at Trevor, not sure what he wants to do, but before I have a minute to think his lips are already on mine and it's not just a mistletoe kiss.

CHAPTER 25

Trevor

Pressing my lips against Eloise's, I feel a surge of electricity shoot through my body. Her face is in my hands, and I'm lost in the moment, forgetting the fact that we have an audience. The cheering and chanting fade away, and it's just the two of us in this moment. But all good things must come to an end, and that end comes in the form of Susie's voice.

"Enough, already," she says, pulling me back away from Eloise.

I tear myself away from the kiss, reluctantly, and glance at Eloise running a gentle finger over her lips, seemingly in shock.

I feel uncomfortable and don't wait for Susie to say anything. I leave the kitchen, feeling like I need to be anywhere but here. The cold winter air hits my face as I step outside, and I take a deep breath, trying to clear my head.

I open the tailgate of the truck and sit on it, facing the town. Despite the daylight, I can still see the town and its surroundings. I'm glad for the moment alone, though it doesn't last. Chase approaches me, jumps on the truck, and takes a seat next to me.

"You okay?" he asks.

"I'm fine."

"What is it about her, bro? I've never seen you this affected by anyone. Not even Maria."

"I'm not affected."

"Sure you're not. Then why are you out here?"

Chase doesn't take his eyes off me. He raises an eyebrow, waiting for my confession.

I take a deep breath and look out towards the town. How do I explain it to Chase? The way Eloise makes me feel is inexplicable. I've never felt this way before. Oh, what the hell. I guess it won't hurt to get this off my chest.

"Fine. She's different."

"Different?" He chuckles. "That's cliché."

"I know."

I can't believe I just admitted that to him. What is wrong with me?

"So what's the problem?"

"It's complicated?"

"What's so complicated about it?"

I take a deep breath before I answer. "Besides the fact that she's Susie's best friend, and I don't want to jeopardize their friendship?"

Chase nods in understanding. "Yeah, aside from that?"

"I don't see how things can work out between us. I like her, but when Christmas is over, and we go back to our lives."

"But you're not going back to a life. You're starting a new one, right?"

"What do you mean. I have a life."

"You had a life in Colorado. You had a business. An apartment. Friends—a life. Now you have destinations."

"That's a life."

"That's escapism."

I let his words hang in the air so as to not absorb them. I don't want to believe what he's saying. Suddenly I realized that I've been after Eloise to let me in and to let everyone know about us. But why? To what end? Am I really ready for anything else? Suddenly this feels too heavy to keep to myself.

"I don't like the way she makes me feel," I confess.

"How's that?"

"Like I could finally be the man Dad wants me to

be."

"Bro, there are worse things in the world than settling down."

On some level, I know he gets it because he went through his rebellious years in high school, and he got to see firsthand what it's like to disappoint Dad. He quickly got over that phase and has been on the straight and narrow ever since. He just finished business school, hence his coming home to help run the family business. He'll be married soon, and eventually start a family following in Mom and Dad's footsteps. And that was never going to be me, at least I didn't think so. I wanted to leave the town I grew up in and make my own way in the world. And I have. So when Eloise makes me feel as though I could just forget who I've been, it makes me want to run and not away, but right into her, it scares the hell out of me.

CHAPTER 26

Eloise

Trevor's kiss has left me stunned, and I struggle to regain my composure. I can feel my heart racing and my knees weakening. I lean against the kitchen counter for support, trying to collect my thoughts. How does he do that? I've been kissed plenty of times before, but never have I felt so overwhelmed and powerless. I take a deep breath and try to shake off the dizziness, but I can't deny the rush of excitement and desire that still lingers within me.

"Sorry about that," says Susie, whipping past me to grab a cup.

I want to say it's okay, but words escape me, and apparently left me silent. I wonder where he went off to. I'm feeling really embarrassed right now, but it seems I have no reason to be. The only one looking at me is Ava, who's quietly clapping her hands in approval, making me feel even more self-conscious.

"Chris would've freaked out if he saw that!" says Susie.

The sound of his name brings me back to the room. And even though I know Trevor's not here, I glance around the room to make sure.

"By the way what did your parents want?" asks Susie.

"My parents?"

"Yeah, didn't you say they called?"

"Oh yeah. I couldn't reach them. My call went to voice mail."

"Lucky you."

"Yeah. Lucky me."

Suddenly, Susie doubles over and clutches her belly. "Ooh, ooh," she says, struggling to catch her breath.

"Another one?" Laura asks, rushing to her side.

"Dave!" Susie calls out, but he's already there offering his support.

"Breathe, baby. You've got this," Dave reassures her in a calm tone.

About half a minute later, Susie's pain dissipates entirely, and she takes a sip of her water.

"It was a strong one," I say. "Maybe more than Braxton?" I ask this time.

She nods. "Oh my god, I don't think I can do this," she tells me. Her eyes filled with terror.

"Of course, you can," I say encouragingly.

"Honey, every woman thinks they can't, until they do," says Laura.

"Eloise, you have to be there when I go into labor. Say you'll be there."

"Really? You want me to be there?" I ask, completely surprised. Instantly I want to cry, and I don't know why.

"Of course, I do. I want Dave, Mom, and you?" she adds.

"Hell, why don't you have the entire family in there with you?" says Grandpa.

I didn't think he was even listening or come to think of it, I didn't even know he was here.

"Of course, I'll be there," I reassure her. We embrace tightly, as if labor is imminent. But I know better, having delivered a couple during my residency, it's unlikely that the baby will arrive tonight.

CHAPTER 27

Trevor

When Chase and I make our way back inside, he goes off to find Ava while I head towards the kitchen. I can hear the loud chatter and laughter from the other rooms, and I crave a moment of solitude. But when I enter the kitchen, I find that I'm not alone. Mom is there, unsurprisingly.

"Hey, honey," she says the moment she hears me come in.

"Mom, you need to get out of this kitchen. Take a break." I take a seat at the island, grabbing an apple to hold me over until I figure out what I want to eat.

"You know I love being here."

"Yeah, I know."

I don't insist that she get out of the kitchen because I know how much being here means to her. It's her sanctuary, her place of solace. Who am I to tell her that this space isn't enough?

This kitchen is where our family gathers, where we connect and bond. As children, we would do our homework at the table during the week, and on the weekends, the same table would host our game nights. It's the heart of our home, and she is the heart of this kitchen.

"That was some kiss," she says, joining me at the island.

"Mom. No."

"Oh, c'mon. We're both adults here."

I can't imagine discussing Eloise with my mom. It's not happening.

"I'll tell you this," she says, sitting down next to me. "She has good taste."

"Mom," I say warning her not to keep going.

"Oh, I'm not talking about you, honey," she replies, waving her hands in the air. "You remember grandma's cookie cutters?"

I nod, unsure of where this is going.

"Out of all the things she could've fallen in love with, in that pantry—and as a baking-lover myself, I know there's plenty in there to love — she fell in love with the one thing that's special in this family. Like I said. Good taste."

"That's great, Mom. But why are you telling me this."

She taps my hand like she's done many times before when words don't seem to get through to me.

"Honey, I've been around you kids long enough to know when there's something going on. And you may not want to talk to your mama about it, and that's fine. But that doesn't mean that I don't want to share what I know to be true."

"And what's that?" I ask with a chuckle because there's no stopping her now.

"That girl likes you. And you better do right by her or Susie's going to be very unhappy with you. You're leaving for Europe in a few days. Does she realize that? If not, better make it clear. That's all I'm saying."

As Mom returns to cutting some produce, I'm left speechless by her comments. It seems like everyone's onto us now. But the truth is, she missed the mark a bit. While Eloise has been receptive to my advances, I'm not entirely convinced that she's into me. My mom has always been a bit blind to my actions, so it's no surprise that she made no mention of my feelings toward Eloise. Has she not noticed that I've been the one pursuing Eloise from the moment I saw her? As it turns out, the apple was enough, so I don't stick around for lunch.

***

A couple of hours pass, and I find myself sprawled out on the couch, tossing a tennis ball in the air out of sheer boredom. The house has become a napping sanctuary, and I can't seem to shake off this sluggishness. It's just me, the tennis ball, and the sound of my own thoughts. That is until Eloise walks in, and I snap to attention. I was starting to think she had joined the nap brigade, but thankfully she's here to save me from my boredom.

She strolls into the living room, her eyes scanning the room for signs of life. "Where is everyone?" she asks.

"Napping," I reply, tossing the tennis ball into the air.

"Really?" she asks.

"Yep," I confirm, glancing at her.

She's changed into a new sweater, this one features a Santa sprawled across a white background. In fact, it's kind of cute. "Nice sweater," I say with a grin.

She folds her arms across her chest, self-consciously.

"I mean it. It looks good on you."

"I didn't peg you for the ugly sweater type."

"Let's just say it's not the sweater I'm into," I say with a wink, dropping the ball.

I take it as my cue to sit up. Plus, I half expect her to run for the door, so I'm up and ready to plead with her to stay if she does. But then she doesn't. She sits across from me, and I watch her carefully, ready for whatever's coming.

"I'm sorry I wasn't honest when we met," she says.

"Just when we met?"

As I meet her gaze, I can sense the weight of her thoughts behind those focused eyes. It's like she's staring into the distance, lost in contemplation.

"Yes, when we met," she confirms.

I'm leaning back on the couch, still fiddling with the ball when I put it down.

"Why are you a doctor?"

"It's rewarding," she says without missing a beat.

"Honesty, Eloise. Is it so hard to just speak what you're really thinking?"

She purses her lips and nervously rubs her hands together, trying to hide the truth. But I don't let her off the hook easily. I wait patiently, silently urging her to open up. Finally, she takes a deep breath and begins to speak, her words flowing out in a torrent. I listen intently, giving her my undivided attention, determined to understand her fears.

"I always thought I would be a doctor. My entire life I've been groomed to be one. And I was okay with it because I lived to please them. But once I entered university, and then medical school I knew I didn't want to live my life that way."

"So quit," I say. As far as I see it, it's that simple.

Eloise looks at me, her expression conflicted. "I was going to," she begins slowly. "Right before starting my residency, I had scheduled a lunch with my parents to tell them I was quitting. Only they surprised me with a house which they bought close to the hospital so that I didn't have to travel too far during late shifts." She starts pacing, clearly agitated. "A house. They bought me a house! I mean who does that?"

I get her because I know the pressures that come with trying to be everything your parents want you to be and falling short.

"It's your life, Eloise. You deserve to go through it however you choose. You didn't ask them to buy you a house. You don't owe them."

"Then why does it feel like I do?" she says, tears welling up in her eyes.

I hate seeing her like this, and I know I have to do something to take her mind off of it, even if just for a little while. "Let's get out of here," I say, taking her hand in mine.

CHAPTER 28

Eloise

I don't know exactly where we're heading, but I'm enjoying being swept away by Trevor. When he opens the door for me to get into the truck, I don't want to let go of his hand. He seems to notice this, and as soon as he gets in, he takes my hand and holds it all the way to town.

"Where are we headed?" I ask curiosity piqued.

"I want to make you smile again and I know what will do the trick."

Despite not knowing where we're going, I feel my lips curve into a smile. His hand is still holding mine, and I give it a gentle squeeze to let him know that I'm on board. He turns to me and flashes that heart-melting smile, complete with a playful wink. I can feel myself getting lost in his charm and I think that I'm in deep trouble.

As soon as we're in town, he parks the car and we quickly get out. He wastes no time speaking up. "This is your last day here. I want you to enjoy everything. It'll be my treat."

I look around, taking in the charming sights and sounds, the colorful storefronts, the twinkle of holiday lights, the smell of freshly baked goods wafting from nearby cafes. I feel a sense of whimsy and excitement bubble up inside me as I turn to Trevor.

"Do you think we can go on a horse carriage ride?" I ask eagerly.

Trevor's face lights up. "Of course, we can!" he says, pulling me close to him. We make our way down the cobblestone streets hand-in-hand, towards the sound of the clip-clop of horse hooves.

There's a short waiting list, so we write down our names and we're told to come back in a couple of hours. It will be dark by then so I imagine it will be even more magical.

"How about some snow tubing?" he asks.

"Snowtubing? They have that here?"

"Oh, yeah. What do you think? You're up for it?"

"Absolutely."

We set off towards a part of town I had yet to

explore. A trolley takes us to the tubing mountain, where we find over 10 lanes to choose from, each beckoning us with its promise of thrilling rides. With only a short line, we excitedly select our tubes and head up, eager to experience the rush of sliding down the mountain.

"You first," I say.

Trevor grabs onto my tube. "Oh we're going down together," he says, then pushes us down the slope without letting go of my tube.

I laugh with every bump and turn. We do it a few more times, until my face feels numb from the cold. When we're done, I'm craving something warm to drink.

"Hot chocolate?" I ask, feeling a warmth in my chest that has nothing to do with the drink.

"Of course," he says.

We approached the booth with our fingers intertwined. A rush of happiness runs through my body at how comfortable his hand feels in mine. We ordered our hot chocolates and found a spot near a fire pit.

Standing there, facing each other, there's a feeling of excitement and nervousness between us. It seems we're both unsure of what to do next, oh so I thought. Surprising me, he takes a step closer to me. His hands are strong yet gentle as he pulls me closer. We lock eyes and I exhale. Before I know it, our lips meet. The world around us disappears, leaving only the two of us in this moment. I run my fingers through his dark hair, feeling the softness of it between my fingers. The kiss deepens, and for a moment, time seems to stand still. When we finally pull away, we're both left breathless and smiling.

"What are you doing to me, Eloise Parker?"

"What am I doing to you?"

"You're making me crazy."

"Good crazy?" I ask.

"Remains to be seen."

Still holding on to my waist, his touch sends shivers down my spine. My arms are wrapped around his neck, pulling him closer as he lays gentle kisses on my lips. I'm floating on a cloud, lost in the moment. It's pure bliss, and I never want it to end.

But we're in public, and the reality of the situation hits us both. We break apart, but he keeps his hand on my waist, still holding me close. I look up at him, lost in his hazel eyes that seem to make me melt every time. He places another tender kiss on my lips before finally pulling back, leaving me breathless and wanting more.

The sun has set and it's almost time to head back for our horse and carriage ride, but before we do, I notice something spectacular. "Is that a light show?" I say, pointing excitedly.

"It is. We can see it if you want. It's on the way."

"I'd love that."

The cool night air is nipping at my cheeks, but I don't mind. I'm too consumed by the warmth of his hand holding mine. The colors of the light show dance in front of us, illuminating our faces and creating a magical atmosphere. We stand there, watching the light show for a while before making our way to the horse and carriage ride.

Trevor's goal was to make me smile, but he's done much more than that. He's given me memories that I'll cherish forever. Our ride is finally ready for us, and I'm about to get in the carriage when they offer us a blanket. "Yes please," I reply.

We're off now, with the occasional jingle of the horse's harness and the crunch of the snow under its hooves as we ride through the town. We pass the quaint little shops and restaurants, while the streetlights cast a warm glow over the town. The snow-covered buildings look like they're straight out of a postcard. Trevor's arm is still around me, and I feel safe, and content nestled under it. Leaning my head on his shoulder feels like the natural thing to do. But in a moment, everything changes. I heard it right away.

Trevor's voice is cautious when he says my name, I sit up and look at him.

"You know I'm leaving, right?" he asks, and my heart sinks at the thought.

"Yeah, I know," I reply, looking at him intently. I wonder where this conversation is headed.

"I don't know what this is," he admits, gazing into my eyes and loosening his arms around me slightly. I hold my breath, waiting for him to continue. But when he doesn't, I reply honestly.

"I don't either," I say, keeping my eyes fixed on him, searching for any clues.

"I just want to make sure we're on the same page," he says, and I feel a knot form in my stomach.

Oh, I understand. He doesn't want it to go any further than this Christmas.

"We are," I say, finally tearing my gaze away from him and pulling away from his embrace.

He takes my not-so-subtle hint and removes his arm completely from me. I'm no longer wrapped in him, and I feel the emptiness he left behind.

My heart aches as I hear his words echo in my mind. A part of me wants to beg him to stay. But I know deep down that it wouldn't be fair. He's the kind of person who lives life on his own terms and I respect that. It's one of the things I admire about him. How can I ask him to give up that part of himself for me? As much as it hurts, I know I have to let him go.

As we drive back to the cabin in silence after the carriage ride, my mind is filled with regret and what-ifs. I replay scenarios in my head, wishing I had been more honest with him from the start.

One Christmas With You

Now I'm just the woman who cheated and lied. The girl who can't stand up for herself or fights for what she wants. Because I do want him more than anything, but I can't even bring myself to fight for him to stay or ask him to choose me. It's a painful realization I'm going to have to live with.

CHAPTER 29

Trevor

The trip into town had accomplished its purpose - it had brought a smile to Eloise's face. However, the blissful moment was fleeting, like a gust of wind that came and went. I had foolishly said something that I shouldn't have, and the smile that had graced her face just moments before slowly dissipated. By the time we returned home, the happy memories we had made during our outing were overshadowed by the tension that now hung heavy in the air. We were back where we started, and I regret my careless words.

I put the car in park, but before I can open the door for her, Eloise is already out of the car. She strides towards the front door, lost in her own thoughts. I hurry to catch up, feeling a pang of guilt in my chest.

As she reaches for the doorknob, I place a hand over hers, stopping her in her tracks. "Hey," I say softly.

She doesn't respond, but also doesn't pull her hand away. She simply turns to face me, her expression unreadable.

"Are we okay?" I ask, my voice laced with concern.

"Why wouldn't we be?" she replies, her tone even.

"I just—" I begin, but Eloise cuts me off.

"Trevor, please," she says, her voice firm but gentle. "We don't need to discuss what we are or what we're not. Because we're nothing. Tomorrow, after Christmas morning, I'll be back home and we'll both be back to our own lives. So, if you're asking if I'm okay with everything that's happened between us, not just this past week but six months ago, rest easy. I'm okay," she says, gesturing for me to remove my hand from hers.

As much as it pains me to admit it, Eloise is right. This is just a fleeting moment, a temporary blip in the grand scheme of things. And when Christmas is over, we'll part ways and likely never see each other again. I knew this but hearing her say it aloud still stings.

Yet, despite knowing that this was never meant to be anything more than a brief encounter, I feel a twinge of sadness at the confirmation of our impending separation. A part of me had secretly hoped that Eloise would tell me that we didn't have to end things, that there was more between us than just a fling, but her words confirm what I already knew—she's just as ready to move on as she was the first time we met.

I push aside my disappointment and force a smile, turning the knob and letting us both in the house. The moment we step inside, we run into Susie who's making her way into the living room.

"Where have you been?" says Susie. "I've been calling you guys all night."

"Sorry, it's my fault. I wanted to show Eloise the town, this time without any distractions. I left my phone in the truck," I say, attempting to take the blame.

"And my phone is on silent," says Eloise taking her phone from her purse. "I'm so sorry," she admits, sounding remorseful.

"Anyway, it's game night, everyone's waiting on—"

She doesn't finish and it takes me a moment to notice why she doesn't.

"Another contraction?" asks Eloise, "Breathe through it," she says, seeing Susie holding her breath.

"Ouch," says Susie, once it's passed. "Why do these hurt so bad?"

"Your body's getting ready for labor."

"Wow, okay. Let's go. We've got a few games going."

Mom, Dad and Grandpa are playing bingo, Dave's shuffling a deck of cards, and Chase, Ava and Maria have a bottle of Whiskey in front of them.

"Not sure taking shots is an appropriate Christmas game," I tell Chase, jumping on the couch next to him.

Eloise doesn't join at first. She stands by Susie and Dave as they start a new card game.

I want to pull my eyes away from her, to just move on with this night and go back to who I was before her. I want to forget that she makes me want to be someone else. But I do none of that.

I'm watching her pretend to be interested in that game, and when Susie and Dave get distracted by an illegal move, she looks over her shoulder at me. I hold her stare, but when Ava starts talking, Eloise turns to her.

"Let's play never have I ever," says Ava.

"Alright, let's do it," says Maria.

"I'm down," says Chase. "How about you?" he asks me.

"Sure, why not," I say, finally looking away from her.

Ava grabs two more glasses from the bar cart, and grabs Eloise by the arm. "C'mon, come play with us."

Eloise allows Ava to direct her wherever she

wants. We're all sitting round the coffee table. Chase is to my left, Maria to my right and Eloise across from me.

"What are we playing?" asks Eloise.

"Never have I ever," says Ava. "Do you know how to play?"

Eloise nods, but her eyes dance around as if she's trying to recall the last time she played.

"I'll go first," starts Chase. "Never have I ever drunk dialed my ex."

Ava and Maria are the only ones to drink.

"Never have I ever gotten a tattoo," says Maria.

"Good one," I say to her, and take a shot.

Eloise glances at my tattoos, then looks away. This makes me smile because I know she likes them.

"Never have I ever broken a bone," says Ava.

Chase broke his leg skateboarding as a kid, so he takes a drink. I drink to that too because I broke a few bones when I had the accident.

None of the women drink.

"Never have I ever had a one-night stand," I say, and take the shot and so does Eloise.

"Whoa, this is getting hot," says Ava.

Eloise avoids my eyes, but it only makes me look at her more.

"Never have I ever gone sky diving," says Eloise.

No one but me drinks.

"Never have I ever cheated on someone," says

Maria.

Only Chase and Ava drink. Though I don't think any less of Chase and Ava for having done so. I'm happy Eloise didn't drink to that one. I can't even imagine her doing something like that.

"You did? Who?" Ava asks Chase.

"Some girl I was dating in college."

"What about you?" he asks her.

"High school beau. I felt awful though. I swore I would never do that again, and I never did."

"Well that's good to know," says Chase.

"Poo bear, I would never cheat on you. I love you."

They're now kissing and we're all uncomfortable.

"Alright, alright," I say, pulling Chase, away.

"Never have I ever been in love," says Maria.

Naturally, Chase and Ava take the shot, and I sit back wanting to be as honest as I can with this silly game.

I take the shot.

Eloise looks at me and takes the shot.

Maria does not.

"Well that sucks," says Maria.

"Aw, sorry babe," says Ava, and crawls over to give her a hug.

Eloise scoots around to get out of her way, and when she does, she turns her gaze to me. Her half smile is filled with regret. Maybe regret for what happened six months ago or what happened here this week. Or maybe for what could be if either of us were willing to admit what we want. But maybe it's for all the things we're not willing to give up. I wish I knew what she's thinking.

CHAPTER 30

Eloise

After game night, I find myself restless trying desperately to fall asleep but it's just not happening. I know what will help. Another cup of hot cocoa will do the trick. It always does.

The house is eerily quiet as I make my way down the stairs, my fluffy slippers padding softly against the floor. I'm dressed in my favorite Christmas pajamas—a cozy white button-down dress adorned with red polka dots. It isn't as festive as some of the other ones in my collection, but it's the comfiest.

The silence extends to the kitchen which is usually a hub of activity. I grab the milk from the fridge and pour it into a red Christmas mug, add the cocoa powder and stick it in the microwave. I know it isn't the ideal way to make hot cocoa, but I don't want to spend too much time on it tonight.

As I wait for the microwave to finish, my mind wanders to the memories I've made during my stay at the cabin. I'll miss this place terribly. I try to picture my next Christmas, but nothing comes close to how I feel about this one. My thoughts drift to Trevor, and I wonder if I'll ever see him again. If I spend Christmas with Susie again, will he be there? Will he be with someone else?

The microwave beeps and I grab the mug, stir it, and head back upstairs, lost in thought. But as I reach the top of the stairs, I'm startled to see Trevor emerging from the bathroom. We both froze, caught off guard by the unexpected encounter.

"Hot cocoa again?" he asks, eyeing my steaming mug.

"Yeah, it helps me fall asleep," I reply, trying to avert my eyes from his damp body.

"Well, goodnight," I mutter, eager to escape the awkwardness.

"Night," he replies, quickly retreating to his own room.

I rush into my room and lean against the door, my heart racing. And that's when I hear it—a faint knock at my door.

I've been here before and know the decision I'll

make in a single moment. My shirt rubs against my skin as shallow breaths escape my lips. With a trembling hand, I grip the knob and turn it, the door slides open. Trevor takes one slow step inside before shutting the door behind him, and I realize there's no going back.

CHAPTER 31

Trevor

Stepping out of the bathroom, I catch sight of Eloise standing in front of me, my heart races with desire. I know I shouldn't let my gaze linger on her for even a moment longer than necessary, but my feet refuse to move. I can feel the heat rising as I force myself to turn away, and head toward my room.

But when I do, I find myself turning around and heading to her room instead. I know I shouldn't be doing this, but the pull toward her is too strong to resist. My heart is racing as I knock softly on her door, hoping she won't hear me, and praying that even if she does, she won't answer. I try to convince myself that I don't want this, that it's a mistake. But I want her, I need her badly.

When she glides the door open, I stop all thinking and I slide inside, shutting the door behind me. My mind is consumed with thoughts of her, of all the things I want to do to her. But I want to go slow, to savour every moment, every touch.

I step toward her, my eyes devouring every inch of her body. She's stunning, breathtaking. I trace the curve of her cheek with my fingertips, and she shivers under my touch.

I want her completely. But I know that I have to be patient and take my time to make sure that every moment is perfect.

As my fingertips trace the lines of her face, her arms hang limply at her sides. She tilts her head back, beckoning me to kiss her. She's giving me full access to her, and I intend to take it. But not quite yet. Despite the overwhelming desire to rip off her clothes, I manage to control myself. The wait will be worth it, for both of us. I slowly graze her lips with mine, teasing her with the promise of a kiss.

I know that I want this, but I also know that I don't want any second thoughts or regrets. Not tonight, not this time. So I take a step back, giving her an out. I should say something to make sure she understands that I'm giving her a moment to walk away. But instead, I go back in and shower her face with soft kisses, showing her how much I want and need her.

It's a delicate dance, a game of patience and control. But I'm willing to play it and do whatever it takes to make her want me as much as I want her.

"Trevor," she whispers.

My hands fall from her face, as her body moves closer and melts into mine. I pull back, giving her another chance to walk away, to tell me to get out. She doesn't.

She hurriedly puts her lips on mine. I let her kiss me until her breath becomes erratic with desperate sighs. I pull away from her, but she's on to me. She bites her lip, taunting me, waiting for me. I devour her body with my eyes.

She doesn't move.

"Come here." I pull her into me and tear her clothes off. I hope she wasn't attached to those pajamas.

I lift her up, wrapping her legs around my waist, and gently lay her on the bed. The sound of her soft moan fills the room, and I can feel the heat rising between us. But before things get too heated, I place my finger over her lips. If we want to keep this between us, she can't make a sound.

"Shh," I whisper, my eyes locked with hers.

She nods in understanding, biting her lip in anticipation. I've teased her enough, and I can feel my own restraint slipping away. I lower myself onto her, feeling her body arch up to meet mine. It's clear that

One Christmas With You

we both want this, and we want it now.

CHAPTER 32

Eloise

Christmas Day

As the sun rises, casting a golden glow through the windows, I open my eyes to see Trevor sitting up. For a moment, I'm disoriented, but then I remember the amazing night we just had. A huge smile spreads across my face.

"It's morning, they'll be up soon," he says, pulling on his pants. But I don't want this moment to end.

I reach for his hand and he looks at me with a grin. The feeling of his warm hand in mine sends a thrill through me and I know I want this to last forever. "Okay," I say, smitten, not wanting to let go.

He leans on the bed, kisses me, and says, "I won't tell Susie. I'll let you."

Without discussing it we both know that we can't keep hiding this from her. "Thank you," I say, feeling grateful that he's giving me the opportunity to speak to her. The anticipation of finally telling her fills me with both excitement and nervousness.

He smiles at me, and I'm struck once again by how handsome he is. I can't imagine a better way to wake up than this, with him by my side.

As he opens the door, he turns back to me and says, "Merry Christmas."

"Merry Christmas," I reply with a joyous grin on my face.

As soon as Trevor leaves, I can't contain my excitement and let out a muffled squeal while throwing the blanket over my head. I feel like I'm floating on cloud nine and nothing can bring me down. Although unsure of what the future holds for us, I know without a doubt that I want to be a part of Trevor's life.

I stay in bed a little longer, reliving the memories of last night and daydreaming about my future with Trevor. Instead of dwelling on potential obstacles, I focus on finding solutions to any challenges that may come our way.

***

Stepping into the living room, I greet everyone with a cheerful "Merry Christmas!"

"Merry Christmas," they say. Everyone, including Trevor is gathered there.

Nothing can wipe away the smile that's still plastered on my face. I've waited for a long time to have a Christmas like this, one surrounded by love and warmth, with people who truly enjoy the holiday. This feels magical, just like it did when I was a kid.

"Come sit, we're getting ready to open presents," says Susie.

I make my way to the couch, feeling grateful to be a part of this.

I take a seat next to Susie and Dave, feeling content but still eager for Trevor's attention. As if reading my mind, he winks at me discreetly and my heart skips a beat.

Trevor is perched on the arm of the couch, where Laura and Mike are sitting. Grandpa is comfortably settled in his recliner, while Ava and Maria occupy the two chairs facing us. Chase is sitting on the floor in front of Ava, beaming with joy. In the midst of this cozy scene, it hits me. I love this family.

"I'll go first. Here, honey," says Laura to Mike after grabbing her gift from under the tree.

Laura excitedly hands the beautifully wrapped

gift, with red wrapping paper and a green bow to Mike. Mike shakes the box as if he could somehow deduce what's inside by sound.

"It's not a rattle," says Grandpa and we all laugh.

Mike doesn't take his time with the paper as I would. Instead, he rips it open then lifts the lid of the box. His mouth drops open.

"Are you kidding me?" he says, closing the box again, as if it's just too much.

"What is it?" asks Chase.

He takes the lid off and turns the box to face us but it's unclear what it is, at least to me.

"A collection of CDs," he says, turning the box for everyone to see.

"Good one," says Trevor.

"Any particular artist"? asks Dave.

"No, just all his favorites," replies Laura, beaming with joy.

"Wow, honey." Mike hugs her tightly, clearly thrilled with his gift.

It's his turn next, he decides, and leans down to grab a gift from under the tree.

"Here's mine. It doesn't compare to yours, but I hope you like it." It's a small box, wrapped with just as much care.

Laura sings with excitement, "What could it be. What could it be." She eagerly opens her gift and takes out the contents, causing her excitement to turn into tears of joy. "Oh, honey," she says, holding the gift close to her heart.

Susie is also eager to see the gift. "Let me see."

"It's a necklace with each of your birthstones," she says, turning to all three of her kids.

"Aw," says Susie, dabbing the corners of her eyes.

I smile at Susie's emotional reaction to Laura's gift. Perhaps it's pregnancy hormones, I think to myself. Trevor seems to share my thoughts as he stifles a chuckle and shakes his head, clearly amused by Susie's response. We exchanged a knowing look.

"Eloise," says Laura, bringing my attention back to her. "I want you to know, that I speak for all of us when I say that we think the world of you. You are part of our family now." She hands me the gift and without warning, I feel emotional.

Laura's words wash over me like a wave of warmth and belonging. Touched by the kindness of her words, tears prickle at the corners of my eyes. As I try to hold them back, I understand how Susie felt moments earlier.

"Thank you, so much," I say.

"Open it," says Trevor.

"Give her a minute, jeez," says Susie, playfully.

The wrapping paper is a beautiful gold color, with a red bow on top. As I always do, I find the taped corners and I lift them gently, making sure not to rip the paper.

It's a medium-sized box with a lid, which I lift to open and when I do, I'm in awe. It's a darling apron inside.

"Oh my god," I say, pulling it out.

My eyes widen in amazement. It's absolutely gorgeous! The fabric has a map outline of Maple Hollow, and my name "Eloise in the Town" is engraved on it.

"This is..." I'm trying to find the words, but nothing seems fitting.

"Epic, isn't it? I knew you would love it," says Susie. "It's from all of us."

"I do. I love it. I really do!" And there's no way I can hold back my tears now. "Thank you, I have something for you too." I grab my gift from under the tree and hand it to Laura.

With the same care and attention to detail, Laura takes her time unwrapping her gift. She delicately removes each piece of tape and slowly peels back the paper, revealing what's inside. As the lid of the box is lifted, I can see the excitement building in her eyes.

Inside the box is a beautifully crafted leather guest book with the words "The Halls Family Cabin" embossed on the cover. I watch as Laura's eyes widen with amazement, and she quickly flips through the pages.

"I signed it," I say, thrilled to have been the first.

"Now this is just perfect," says Laura showing it

to the rest of the family.

My heart swells with happiness as the family passes around the guest book. Susie remarks on how cool it is and expresses her surprise that they never thought to get one before.

I steal a glance at Trevor, and he looks at me with pride and appreciation. It's as if he knows that I found the perfect gift for his family. As the book is being passed around, Chase eagerly makes an announcement.

"Okay, I guess it's my turn," says Chase, standing.

I notice Trevor's sudden change in posture as he stands up and crosses his arms. His expression is difficult to decipher, and I'm left wondering if he's feeling impatient or nervous. Regardless, his demeanor has definitely shifted.

Chase lets out a deep breath as he approaches Ava and takes her hand, prompting her to stand. My heart races as I realize what's happening.

With a beaming smile, Chase looks up at Ava and says, "Ava, you have been a light in my life from the moment we met, and I want your light to be with me for the rest of my days." The women in the room let out an audible gasp, with Ava's reaction being the most obvious. As he begins to kneel, the anticipation in the room is palpable.

"Ava, will you make me the happiest man in this in this world and marry me?" His voice is shaking with emotion as he looks up at Ava with a wide grin. He's holding out a small velvet box and opens it to reveal a glittering diamond ring inside. Ava is covering her mouth with her hand, tears of joy streaming down her face as she nods her head yes.

"Yes!" she finally squeals, jumping into his arms.

Since Maria was right next to her, she is the first to congratulate her. Then, Laura, Susie and then me.

"Congratulations," I say, hugging and feeling a close connection to this woman I met only two days ago.

"Thank you," she says, hugging me as if I'm the one who's getting married. "We're going to be sisters-in-law, I just know it," she whispers.

I squeeze her and smile, then let her go for the others to have their moment with her.

No one can hold back their excitement as they congratulate Chase and Ava. Suddenly, I'm struck with an idea. Clearing my throat, I stood trying to get everyone's attention. "Excuse me, everyone," I say, my voice ringing through the room. "I would love to cook everyone a celebratory breakfast to mark this special day. Laura, if it's alright with you, I would like to take over the kitchen for the morning."

Laura's face lights up with a smile. "It's more than alright," she says. "I'm grateful for the offer."

"Thank you," I reply, already starting to plan out the menu in my head.

CHAPTER 33

Trevor

Eloise is busy in the kitchen preparing breakfast, and while I wanted nothing more than to join her, I promised to give her time to talk with Susie. But after last night, it's difficult to stay away from her. So here I am, sitting in my truck outside, counting down the minutes until I can be alone with her again. The anticipation is almost unbearable, but I know it will be worth it once it's all out in the open.

This Christmas, I purchased a gift for everyone, but there's still one left. I enlisted Grandpa's help on it. I told him exactly what I wanted, and he ran with it. It required a visit to the shop, so he snuck away yesterday for a couple of hours to get it done for me. This morning, he handed it to me before Eloise got downstairs.

I couldn't give the gift to her in front of everyone for fear it would put our secret on display. Grandpa's the only one who knows about us because, well, he knew from that first moment he saw me and Eloise together, or so he told me.

It seems I'm at a crossroads. The last time I sat on this truck I was sure I wasn't going to give up my plans for Eloise. I wasn't going to change who I've been for someone I barely knew. But everything's different now. She's no longer running away from me. I feel like we have a future together and I want it. I want it more than anything else I've ever wanted. My body yearns for her, so I decide to go inside to be near her, but just as I'm about to stand, Dad joins me.

"Hey, son."

"Hey."

"How about that proposal, huh?" he says, leaning on the truck.

"Yeah. Pretty nice."

"Yeah," he repeats in a drawn-out sigh.

There's a conversation brewing inside his head, so I wait for it to fully form.

"So he told you?"

And there it is.

I know exactly where he's going with this.

"That he's coming back home to join the business?" I ask.

"Yep. That's nice, don't you think?"

"It is Dad. I'm happy for both of you. I know having your sons, or at least one of your sons, in business with you means everything to you."

"Yeah, yeah it does," he says, looking out, thinking again.

I suspect he doesn't want to say something that will send me running away. I haven't been easy, and I know it. It's time I acknowledged that.

"Hey Dad."

He turns to me, lips pursed, holding back something.

"I'm sorry I can't be who you want me to be."

He looks down, then away. I see him swallow words, feelings, thoughts, maybe a combination of it all and I feel for him.

"Son, you're exactly who I raised you to be'— independent, self-sufficient, a go-getter with the kindest of hearts. Though that last one might have something to do with your mom," he says, laughing and nudging me with his shoulder.

"Really? What about my tattoos, college, my career, my business, Europe?" I say, unclear as to why he's had a sudden change of heart.

"Sure, sure. I wish some of those things hadn't happened or maybe happened differently. Like why an entire arm of tattoos? Why not just one?" he asks.

I shrug my shoulders because I have no answer

for that.

"And college, sure, it would've been nice if you went to my alma mater, but those things don't really matter, not in that grand scheme of life."

"Why now?"

"Did you see us in there today? We're blessed. And yes, I worry about you but not because you're doing something I disapprove of but because you're different and sometimes I don't understand. And that doesn't mean you're wrong or, hell, that I'm wrong. Anyways, I just want you to know that I love you. And I hope you have a good trip."

"Thanks Dad."

We both stand and hug, and it's the first time we've connected like this in a long time.

"I want you to know that I hope to have a life just like yours one day. Family, kids, the whole shebang," I tell him.

He pulls me in for another hug and pats me hard on the back. Something tells me he never expected those words from me. And if I'm honest, neither did I.

"Let's get inside, I was supposed to let you know that breakfast was ready."

CHAPTER 34

Eloise

We're all sitting around the table having breakfast, but Trevor and Mike are nowhere to be seen. I want to ask where they are, but I know it's not my place, especially since I haven't talked to Susie yet. I was so busy cooking breakfast that I didn't really have a moment to chat with her. Besides, she was distracted talking to Ava about wedding and baby themes.

The French toast I made seems to be a hit, but I'm not surprised—they loved the pancakes I made as well. I'm sitting across from Susie and next to Ava, with an empty seat next to me. I'm glad because it's the only place for Trevor to sit, if he ever decides to show up for breakfast. Where is he? This is what he does to me, he makes me crazy. It's not enough to just be in the same vicinity as him, I need him near me.

Finally, he and Mike come in and Trevor goes straight for the empty chair next to me.

"Hey," he says, putting a hand on my thigh, and doesn't move it.

I jump, startled by his boldness, and everyone notices.

"Chills," I say, pointing to my neck.

Trevor chuckles, as I try to hold back my own laughter.

I haven't really touched my breakfast and it seems impossible to do so now—with his hands on me. He, however, has no problem eating. I have a choice to make here, place my hand on his, which is what I want to do or give him a taste of his own medicine.

I grab the napkin, wipe my mouth as if I've just taken a bite, and then pretend I'm bringing it to my lap. It's an excuse to look down and situate my hand exactly where I want it. On his thigh, but not as close to the knee as he has his.

On cue, he lets out a choking cough.

"You, okay?" asks Laura.

"Fine," he muffles, clearing his throat.

We exchange looks and images of last night swirl around me. He lifts his hand off my thigh, and I do the same. It's too much for Christmas morning and breakfast with the family.

No one gets up from the table when they're done eating. I've noticed this trend with them. This is when and where they catch up. At my family's table, we do all the talking while we're eating, and when we're finished, we make a dash for it. Dad's always the first to go. Once he's gone, Mom sees no point in sitting around anymore, she stands up and waits for me to do the same. It's nice that they're not desperate to leave each other's company.

"So Trevor, how long are you gonna be gone for?" asks Mike.

This question brings me back to the present.

"Not sure."

"You don't have a plan? Or places you've booked?" continues Mike.

"No. Plans change," he says, eyeing me from the corner of his eye, turning the corners of his lips up. It's discreet enough that only I notice.

"Well, I'm going to be a nervous wreck the entire time you're gone. You make sure you call me now and then," says Laura, holding back tears.

"Mom he'll be fine," says Chase.

"Call me when you get there, maybe I'll meet you for a week or so," says Maria. "I've always wanted to go."

"That would be nice," says Laura.

Trevor doesn't say yes or no to Maria, but his

hand has landed on my knee this time, and he squeezes it, and rubs it as if to say I have nothing to worry about. I put my hand on his and intertwined our fingers.

"Eloise are you ready for work tomorrow?" asks Susie.

Uh-oh.

My hand unlaces from Trevor's, and I sit up ready to stop her if this question leads to Chris.

"Ready as I'll ever be." We haven't talked about work the entire time we've been here and it's not something I want to discuss. It will inevitably give me away.

Susie not liking Chris has worked in my favor the entire time I've been here. But this was too close. I have to talk to her before she says something. It's now or never. The family's involved in separate conversations, and Susie's just listening to all of it. I make my move.

"Sus," I say.

She turns to me. "Yeah."

"I'd love a moment alone." I motion toward the kitchen.

She seems surprised, but she doesn't make a big deal about it, or question me. She simply stands and follows me. We're just about to enter the kitchen when...

"What is happening?" she cries.

"Oh, no," escapes my mouth.

"My water just broke," she says turning back to the table.

CHAPTER 35

Trevor

The first thing I do when Susie tells us her water broke is reach for my camera and snap one photo of her. When I look at what I captured it's hilarious. It's one of those gasping moments, where everyone's in a panic including the woman in labor. She might not appreciate it at first, but one day it will be one of her favorite pictures.

When Eloise asked to speak with Susie, I knew this was the moment she was going to tell her about us. Finally. No more sneaking around or pretending we're just friends. But I don't even have to ask if Eloise told her because they hadn't even reached the kitchen when Susie was already back.

Now, we're in separate cars following Dave and

Susie in their minivan to the closest hospital in town, which is thirty minutes away. Eloise rode with Susie for many reasons, but most of all because Susie was a nervous wreck. I suppose having a doctor next to her offered a level of comfort that none of us could provide.

I chose to drive alone because I wanted to bring my truck. If I'm honest, I was thinking ahead. When this is all over, Eloise will need a ride to the cabin, and I want to be the one she rides back with.

The ride alone gives me the time I need to think things through. Eloise and I haven't exactly talked about plans for the future. Is there even a future for us, even a near future? I still intend on going to Europe, but for how long? Initially, I had no time limit. I was going to be there for as long as I wanted, but since I'm already planning my trip back just to be with Eloise, I'm thinking I won't be there as long as I originally thought.

Then what? Will I move back here, to Georgia to be with her? I would. But is that something she even wants? Sorting this out, going through traffic, steering through snow and without Eloise to bounce ideas off of seems pointless, if not dangerous. I could be making too much of us but my gut tells me that I'm not.

I saw Eloise's face when Maria suggested I call her to meet up in Europe. She didn't seem happy about that and I don't blame her. If someone had said that to her, I wouldn't have been able to pretend that I was okay with it. I quickly push that thought away. The idea of Eloise being with someone else is not something I want to think about.

It took thirty-five minutes to get to the nearest hospital, ten minutes to find parking and another fifteen for everyone to check in at the front desk. We're all gathered in the waiting room, waiting for either Eloise or Dave to come give us an update, but most importantly to get Mom to see Susie before she loses her mind.

This is my first time in the maternity ward and the vibe here is very different. Though I can't say the overall scent isn't the same.

Sitting is too difficult to do right now, and pacing will just drive Mom crazy so I'm leaning against the wall, resisting the urge to leave. I've had my fair share of hospitals in my lifetime, and although by all accounts this is a happy hospital visit, I'd still rather be anywhere else. I know exactly why Eloise doesn't want this to be her life. Though I have immense appreciation for what she does, I can't imagine the kind of pain doctors encounter daily.

We're not exactly in a private waiting room, but we are alone except for the various doctors and nurses that keep walking by. We've been waiting for about 20 minutes when Eloise finally comes out.

Mom is the first to rush to her. My first instinct is to go to her but I stop myself. I let her update Mom and Dad because they need it most.

"She's doing well. She's 6 cm dilated, and 90 percent effaced."

"Oh my God." Mom can hardly contain herself and she leans on Dad for support.

"What does that mean?" asks Dad.

"It means baby is definitely coming. She seems to be dilating pretty quickly which is rare for first time moms but she's doing wonderfully."

There's no denying that Eloise has her doctor hat on. She's carrying a confidence I haven't seen in her before. I never would have guessed that she hates this. It suits her.

"So, I can go in, right?" asks Mom.

Eloise has just spotted me, and we lock eyes. It's hard to resist looking at her the way I do. I've been trying to do a good job, especially around the family but at other times it's not possible. She's watching me carefully, trying to sort out what I'm thinking. I'll fill her in later when I ask her to put her doctor's hat back on.

"Eloise?" Mom asks again.

"Yes, of course," she says, half distracted by me. "Right through there, just let them know who you're seeing, and they'll let you in," she says, already walking toward me.

I push off the wall, walking toward her when she starts talking.

"What are you doing?" she asks, a smile curving on her lips.

"What?" I ask, pretending I have no idea what she's referring to.

"What if your family saw the way you were looking at me," she half whispers.

Grandpa is reading his book, Chase, Ava and Maria are on their phones.

"Who? Them?" I say, pointing to them.

"Just keep it together."

"I can't help that I liked what I saw?"

"And what's that?" she says, putting a strand of hair behind her ear.

"Your doctor's voice."

She suppresses a laugh.

"Come with me," I say, taking her hand.

I find a quiet corner of the floor where I think we can sneak in a moment of privacy. I pull her close and plant a soft kiss on her lips. She hesitates at first, her hand on my chest, but soon melts into my embrace.

"Trevor. They will see us?" she whispers, breaking away.

"So what?" I reply, grinning as I lean in for another kiss.

However, our moment is short-lived, as we're interrupted by a sudden call of her name. "Eloise?!"

The voice echoes through the room, snapping us back to reality.

Eloise pushes me away, and her body stiffens in response. I glance over to see who interrupted us, but I don't recognize the person. Eloise, on the other hand, seems to know exactly who it is.

CHAPTER 36

Eloise

No, not now. Not when I'm so close to figuring things out with Trevor. My mind is racing as I look back and forth between Chris and Trevor, trying to process what's happening. I can't find my words. This isn't happening.

"Eloise?" Chris says again, breaking the awkward silence.

"Who is this?" Trevor demands, his gaze locked onto Chris.

Wake up Eloise! Speak! Find that voice Trevor was just talking about and speak up for yourself. "Chris," I say to both of them.

"Who the hell is Chris?" asks Trevor, looking back

and forth between us.

"Her boyfriend of two years. Well, ex-boyfriend," he corrects.

"What are you doing here?" I ask, as if it matters. As if that's the problem.

"So this is why you missed Christmas with your family, for this low life."

Trevor looks him up and down and lets out a humorless laugh. For a minute I think he's going to come at Chris. But he doesn't. He does the one thing I don't want him to do. He turns to walk away.

"Trevor," I say, grabbing his arm.

He stops but doesn't look at me.

I don't let go of his arm for fear he'll leave, but I do turn to face him, even if he can't bear to look at me, "Please don't go. I can explain."

"We're over Eloise, you hear me. Good luck keeping your residency now," says Chris.

Trevor turns and starts walking toward him.

"Hey, back off man. I can have you arrested like that," says Chris, snapping his finger.

This doesn't stop Trevor. The only thing that does is me, standing between them.

"Chris it's over. It's been over," I yell.

"You bet it is," he says, eyeing Trevor carefully.

"You know what? No, he's not the reason I didn't spend Christmas with you. You're the reason I didn't spend Christmas with you. Remember six months ago, Chris," I say, anger flooding my senses. "When you went to Hawaii, on a medical retreat? I went to meet you there, to be with you. And you know what I saw? You with another woman."

Chris eyes widen, seemingly more stunned by this admission than seeing me with Trevor.

"No, you didn't," he says, denying the truth.

"Ah, you didn't think I knew, right?

I've let go of Trevor and I'm practically in Chris's face.

"And yeah, I spent Christmas with him," I say, pointing back to Trevor, but without taking my eyes off Chris. "And I would do it one hundred times over." I pause to form the words clearly and when I have them, I continue. "You, cheating on me six months ago was the best thing that ever happened to me because I met him." When I turn to look at Trevor, he's not there.

I'm shattered.

I moved away from Chris and looked down the hall, but he's gone. I leave Chris behind, not bothering to explain anything else. It's Trevor I owe an explanation to. I ran back to the waiting room, but he was not there.

"Has Trevor been here?"

"No," says Mike.

"Thought he was with you," says Chase.

I'm halfway in the room but then I take off again

to find Trevor.

The hospital is not as big as the one I work at, but it's big enough. He could be anywhere. But if I've learned anything about Trevor these last few days, it's that he runs to his car when he needs to be alone. I make a dash for the garage.

I don't know this hospital as well as I know mine, but I've been here a few times. It's almost where I did my residency.

I find an elevator that takes me to the garage, and I frantically get in and press the fifth-floor button. The hospital was busy when we got here, it's likely he didn't find parking on the lower levels.

I'm alone for only one floor, then a couple comes in.

They smile politely, and I attempt a forced smile that I'm not sure even makes it to my face.

They get off on the fourth floor and it feels like they're sloths, but then again so do the elevator doors. I push the close button over and over again willing it to shut faster. *Hurry up.*

When I reach the fifth floor, I don't wait for the doors to fully open. I'm off and running, bumping into a family that was waiting outside.

"Sorry," I say, already too far for them to hear.

I assess the garage before I make another move. I need to find him and don't have a lot of time. I glance at every corner of the garage without going too far, and that's when I see him. He's on the rooftop, sitting in the back of his truck.

CHAPTER 37

Trevor

I'm only sticking around for Susie's sake. If I were to leave now, just before the baby comes, she would never forgive me. And honestly, I wouldn't blame her. But I can't bear to spend one more second inside that hospital. The sterile smell, the sounds of machines beeping, the sight of Eloise—it's all too much for me to handle. I needed to get out, take a walk, clear my head.

I'm sitting in my truck, taking in some much-needed fresh air. The snow has stopped, but the wind is blowing hard, making it brutally cold outside. Nonetheless, it's better than being inside the hospital. I had planned on giving Eloise her Christmas present after she told Susie about us. I had hoped it would happen at some point today, so I brought it with me. But now, I'm holding it in my hand, feeling like a fool. I want to slam it on the ground or throw it away, but I haven't. Instead, I'm holding it and turning it in my hands, knowing it's the only good piece of her that I have left.

My mind is processing everything that just went down when I hear Eloise say my name.

"Trevor."

I'm not ready to talk to her or see her for that matter.

"Save it," I say, without looking at her.

"Let me explain," she pleads.

I sneer at her approach.

"Please look at me," she asks.

I don't.

"Honesty is the one thing I ever asked you for," I reminded her.

I hear her footsteps drawing nearer.

"I know. It just got so complicated," she says, but her words feel empty.

She's close to me now but I don't want her to be, so I stand and step away from her, gift still in hand.

"How much did you hear back there? I turned around and you were gone."

My jaw clenches before I answer.

"I heard enough."

"Trevor. I never wanted to lie."

I chuckled again because that's all she's done since we met.

"I know what it looks like. But I was planning on breaking up with him. Did you hear that?" she says, her voice getting impatient.

I turn to face her for the first time.

"No. You don't get to do that. You don't get to play the victim here."

"I'm not. I'm only trying to explain."

"Explain what? That you were planning on breaking up with your boyfriend? Do you hear how ridiculous that sounds?" Tell me, when were you planning on doing that? The first time we slept together, or the second, or maybe the third?" I say, frustration rising in me. "Should I go on?"

"I.. I.." she stutters. "I know how it sounds but I swear it's not that cut and dry."

"I think it is."

"We were done way before I met you."

"Except you weren't," I yell, stepping back, further away from her. "Yeah, I heard. He cheated on you, and you thought it would be okay to get back at him with me, right?"

"It wasn't like that!"

"Eloise, please just go. I don't ever want to see you again."

"Trevor, please." Her voice quivers, and even without looking at her, I know she's crying.

I turn my gaze and walk up to her. She doesn't try to hide her tears. She just lets them fall. I won't be as cruel to her as she's been to me. I won't give her false hope. No, I won't do that to her. I'm inches from her, even though I don't want to be.

"Save your tears, Eloise, because they mean nothing to me. See, before this, your tears would've broken me I would've moved heaven and earth to make you happy. Instead, all I'm left with is who I thought you were, who I hoped you would be, and who you really are. Merry Christmas," I say, handing her the gift in my hand before turning and walking away.

I don't want to hear her excuses anymore. *I don't care*. This is all I say until I take the stairs to the ground floor, and cross the street to a coffee shop. I text Chase and ask him to let me know when the baby arrives.

CHAPTER 38

Eloise

When he walks away, I don't move. People walk by me on their way to their cars and stare as they do. To them it might seem as though the bitter winter has me frozen in place. But this chill is nothing compared to Trevor's icy words. I grip my chest with my free hand and hold his gift in the other. I've lost him, just when I... I can't even admit the words to myself. I'm afraid if I do, I will collapse right here. But it's no use. My heart knows it. My body knows it. I love him and I've lost him.

I look down at the gift he placed in my hands. Tears blur my vision, but I can't bring myself to look away from the box. It's wrapped in bright red paper with a green ribbon tied around it, and it seems to mock me with its cheery colors.

My fingers fumble around the edges of the tape, trying to find a way to peel it back without destroying the wrapping paper. I'm careful not to damage it, as if preserving it will somehow preserve the memory of what Trevor and I once had. The paper gives way with a soft rip, and I'm left staring at the box in my hands.

The wind has picked up, and a gentle snow has started to fall again, but I make no attempt to get out from the cold. With the back of my hand, I wipe the tears that have fallen. Pulling the gift out, I'm careful with the wrapping paper. Unlike me, it's still intact and I want to keep it that way.

With trembling hands, I lift the lid of the small box and gaze at the contents inside. It's a delicate, wooden ornament, carved with the intricate details of Laura's tree cookie cutter. My heart swells with emotion as I realize the significance of this gift. It's an exact replica of the tree cookie cutter that has been passed down in his family for generations. I take it out of the box by the string and hold it in front of me. The wind picks up and the ornament moves in my hand, almost as if it's dancing with joy.

Tears stream down my face, as I press the ornament against my chest because I know I will cherish it for as long as I live. Suddenly I realized I've been gone too long, and I need to get back to Susie. I put the carved ornament in one pocket of my coat and the box and wrapping paper in the other.

Trevor didn't return to the hospital, so I took the elevator back to the maternity ward and stopped at the restroom to freshen up before facing Susie. I quickly check my reflection in the mirror to make sure my makeup is either gone or still intact. It's gone, but I don't mind. As I try to fix my hair, I realize that the real mess is on the inside, and there's no fixing that.

Susie will be able to tell I've been crying, she always does. But I can blame it on the excitement of it all. Another lie. Why not?

She's in the middle of a contraction when I come in, so she doesn't notice me at first. Dave is holding her hand, while Laura stands by, hands clasped together seemingly holding back tears. Susie's pain is her pain. A rush of emotions hit me at once. Tears well up again and I can't pretend they're not there.

"Hey," says Susie, contraction over. She stretches her hand for me to come. "What's the matter?"

"Nothing. Nothing." I wipe the tears from my face and hold her hand.

"Honey, I'm going to give the family an update. Don't you go having that baby before I get back?" says Laura.

"She's doing great," says Dave. "We're almost there. eight cm dilated and 99% effaced.

"Good. Good," is all I can say.

Susie eyes me wearily. She knows something's up. But then she has another contraction and she's focused on her own pain.

I do what I'm supposed to do for her, keep track of the contraction on the monitor and remind her when it's almost done.

We do this for another three hours until it's finally time for her to push. Dave takes one side, and Laura the other, while I stand close enough for her to feel my support.

After almost an hour of pushing, the exhaustion is visible on her face. But when it's finally over, all the pain and fatigue are forgotten in an instant. The cries of her perfect, beautiful daughter fill the room and we all burst into tears of joy.

While Susie gets settled into a room, Laura and I join the family. It will likely be an hour or so before they can see her and meet the baby. Trevor's not here and I don't know if I'm relieved, or sad about it. On the one hand I want to see him and tell him how much I loved his gift, but on the other, I can't bear to be on the receiving end of his icy demeanor again. Yeah, it's much better that he's not here.

I have been sitting in the corner for the past hour, quietly answering some medical questions from Ava who seems to be unexpectedly fascinated with medical jargon. Everyone else is busy talking about the baby, so Trevor's absence seems to have escaped their attention for now.

Feeling overwhelmed by my own thoughts, I desperately search for a distraction. My phone is within reach, so I grab it, but as soon as I do a new wave of anxiety washes over me. I see that I have five missed calls from my mom.

I forgot to call for Christmas.

Calling them seems like the right thing to do so I step out of the waiting room to make the call, but when I do, Trevor is stepping off the elevator. And instinctively I move toward him. I want to thank him for the gift.

He looks down at me icily, unmoved by my presence.

"I know you don't want to talk to me. But I just want to say thank you. The gift is more than I could've ever imagined. And I love it."

He glares at me, but not with the same intensity as before. Perhaps he's not as angry anymore.

"You're welcome," he says and moves around me to the waiting room.

I turn to look at him, hoping he looks back, but he doesn't. Instead of calling my mom, I head toward where Susie is recovering, and I use my doctor's status to get in before anyone else.

As expected, I got in without any problems. I still have about fifteen minutes before they let the rest of the family in, so I have to talk fast.

"Hey," I say, quietly entering.

"Hey, she says, looking up. She's feeding the baby with a bright smile on her face.

Dave is standing close by watching them both with such glee, it's contagious.

"She's beautiful," I say, smiling.

"Isn't she?" she says.

The three of us are fixated on the baby's face, captivated by her angelic beauty. I clear my throat, attempting to steady my voice. As I prepare to speak, a tightness grips it, knowing the conversation that lies ahead. It's surreal to think that I was present for her birth and that for a brief moment, I allowed myself to believe that I could be a permanent part of their lives.

"What's wrong?" she asks.

I look between her and the baby, and it seems impossible that I would ruin this moment for her.

"Nothing. I.. I.. have to go back to work. So I'm leaving. I just wanted to say goodbye."

"Oh, no. But it's Christmas."

"I know. It's okay. I've had the best Christmas of my life. I want you to know that. I'm so grateful to you and your family."

"Thanks, but you're being weird. I'll be back home in a few days. You have to come by."

I simply nod, my sorrow choking me. This might very well be the last time I see her. I want to come clean and explain myself, but she matters more at this moment.

"I'll see you okay," I say, "Bye, Dave."

"Oh, wait, I can't believe I didn't tell you," she says. "Want to know what we named her?"

"Of course."

"Eloise," she says, with a smile that brightens the room. It makes me think of Trevor.

"Oh, Susie. I'm so honored."

Now it's impossible to hold back the tears, so I don't. I make it out right before the family is allowed in. I call a cab and have them take me to the nearest car rental.

CHAPTER 39

Trevor

This Christmas has been more than I ever hoped for and more than I wanted. I'm thrilled about the birth of my first niece and I'm grateful that it all went well. But my heart is broken more than I care to admit.

We all spill into Susie's hospital room, excited to see the new addition to the family. Eloise wasn't with us in the waiting room, and I expected her to be here with Susie, but she's not. And, I'm not the only one to notice her absence.

"Where's Eloise," asks Ava.

"Oh, she got paged. She had to go back to work, didn't she tell you?" says Susie.

"Oh, no," she says, seeming disappointed.

"She didn't say goodbye?" asks Susie.

"No. I'm surprised," says Mom.

"Well, that's not like her," says Susie. "Did something happen?" she asks, looking at all of us.

"No. I don't think so," says Mom.

"That's strange. I'll call her later. Something was definitely wrong with her when she left."

"Maybe Trevor knows?" says Grandpa.

I exhale in frustration and remember where I'm at, and what we're doing here. Celebrating Susie and her newborn. This is no place for my drama.

"I have no idea," I say, not making eye contact.

But when I lift my eyes, I see Susie staring at me.

She senses something, but for the time being she doesn't say anything. She lets the Grandparents enjoy the moment and happily chats with Ava.

"Are you guys ready to learn her name?" asks Susie with giddy excitement.

"We sure are. We can't keep calling her baby," says mom taking her turn holding her.

"Eloise," she announces.

I look toward the door, expecting to see her. But it takes me no time to realize I've missed it entirely. My sister has named her baby Eloise. Great!

"What do you think, Trev?" asks Susie, eyeing me carefully.

"I like it," I say.

But she squints at me, just like when we were kids, and she knew I was up to no good. And just like then, I averted her stare at all costs.

***

A short half hour later, we're saying goodbye. It's time to let Susie and Dave enjoy their new baby. And it's time for all of us to go back to the cabin. That cabin holds an entirely new memory now, and it will be difficult to return to it. Her absence will be felt.

"Hey, Trev, can you hang back a moment," says Susie, just before I get to the door.

"Sure."

"Honey, will you give me a moment with Trev?" she asks Dave.

"Sure. I need to move the car anyway."

It was the moment Eloise had dreaded ever since she realized that I was her best friend's brother. I now know that she was afraid Susie would reveal the fact that she had a boyfriend.

"What's up," I ask, standing but ready to dash.

"Sit," she says, pointing to the chair.

I turn it around so that I'm facing the back then sit and wait for her to speak.

"What's going on between you and Eloise."

"Nothing."

"Did you both think I was stupid? You guys have

been giving each other googly eyes from the moment I introduced you to each other."

I let out an exhausted breath.

"What happened?"

"Did you know she had a boyfriend?"

"That jerk? Yeah. What about him?"

I go on to tell her everything that happened, minus the intimate details, of course. But I do tell her how she snuck away after our first time together, and how she continually lied to me.

"There must be some explanation. Why didn't she tell me he cheated on her?" she says, confused.

"I don't know."

"Well, what are you going to do?"

"About what?"

"About her. You're not going to let this get between you two, are you?"

"There is no us. It's over."

"You can't be serious."

"As a heart attack."

"Well, you know what? It's your loss. Eloise is the kindest, most generous person I know. And any guy would be happy to have her."

The mere thought of another man having her, makes me crazy. But with time, I'll get over it. I just have to.

"And," she continues her rant. "I for one am glad she ended things with that jerk. He's an awful human."

Again, the thought of Eloise being with him, treating her badly makes me want to find him and put him through a wall. But I remind myself that she's no longer my problem.

"So what? You're still leaving then?"

"Like I said. Whatever could've been, is over now. She'll go back to her life, and I'll go back to mine as if we never happened."

"Except you did, and no amount of running is going to change that."

Running. There it is again. I'm not running, I think for the hundredth time. I'm living my life on my terms.

"Fine. I love you no matter what. And if you ever change your mind, know that I'm okay with the two of you."

"Noted."

As I get back on the road and leave the hospital behind, my mind is racing. I can't shake off the feeling of disappointment and betrayal. The drive back to the cabin feels very different to the drive into the hospital. Instead of dreading the idea of leaving, I'm now consumed by the urgency of it. The sooner I leave, the better. The road stretches out ahead of me, winding through the countryside. The trees sway in the wind, as if they too are beckoning me to leave this place. My thoughts swirl around like the leaves caught in the gusts of wind, until I finally reach the cabin.

CHAPTER 40

Eloise

My mind raced for the two hours it took to get home. Now, I'm in bed, in my pajamas after taking a long bath. I haven't stopped thinking about Trevor, Susie, and her family. I left without saying goodbye or giving any explanation. They must think I'm the worst person in the world. After they welcomed me into their home and family this Christmas, I didn't have the decency to even thank them. I miss them already.

The truth is I couldn't face them or Trevor. I couldn't bear Trevor looking at me the way he did, I would've broken down in front of them all. They deserve to preserve their happy day.

My home is a stark contrast to the cabin,

reminding me that I didn't have the time, or rather, didn't make the time to decorate it this year. I long for the cozy ambiance of the cabin, where the sound of laughter and voices filled every corner. Most of all, I miss the butterflies in my stomach that came with being around Trevor.

I tuck the blanket close to my chest, remembering the sensation of his touch on my skin. I miss being wrapped in his embrace. My body aches for him, and I'm painfully aware of his absence. But it's not just my body that yearns for him; my heart and mind do too. I was unaware of how much I needed what he offered me until it was no longer there.

I've been driving myself crazy thinking about him all day, and I don't want to continue torturing myself. I look for anything to distract me once again. I grab my phone and make the call I've been avoiding all day.

As soon as Mom answers the call, I can tell from the tone of her voice that something is off.

"Hello Eloise," she says, and I can almost hear the disappointment dripping from her words.

"Merry Christmas, Mom," I reply tentatively, wondering how much she knows.

"Well, it's about time," she retorts. "Christmas is almost over. Not to mention that Chris called your father and told him everything you've been up to."

I feel my stomach drop at the mention of Chris's name, but I try to keep my voice steady. "Mom—"

"Eloise, you need to come over and explain yourself."

I'm not surprised Chris called and told them about Trevor. I don't have the strength to lie or even argue with her request.

"In a couple of days. I work tomorrow and the day after."

"When, Eloise?"

"New Year's Eve."

"Very well, see you then," she says and hangs up without waiting for me to reply.

I didn't bother sitting up as we talked. Instead, I lay on the bed with my head on the pillow, too exhausted to put forth the effort. I wish I could call Trevor and hear his voice just one more time. My thoughts drift to Susie and her beautiful baby and the honor she gave me by naming her after me.

I'm startled when my phone rings, and I jump. I'm hoping it's Trevor. Maybe he's changed his mind. Thought things through and is willing to put things behind us. But it's Susie.

It rings and rings. And no matter how many times I try to slide to answer, I can't. Immediately after, a text message comes through.

Susie: Call me when you get this. We need to talk.

My heart sinks. Though it may seem

insignificant, the absence of an emoji in her text confirms what I had feared all along. Susie is not okay with what had happened between Trevor and me, and she probably knows about what happened with Chris by now. Susie never sends a text without an emoji; it's just not like her. I wouldn't be surprised if she has already changed the baby's name to something else.

It's all too much. I turn my pillow over because my tears have dampened it. My only prayer tonight is that I don't dream of Trevor.

CHAPTER 41

Trevor

Finally, Christmas is over, and my flight is just a couple of days away. I'm counting down the minutes until I can leave. Currently, I'm holed up in the cabin behind closed doors while the rest of the family is downstairs. Earlier today, I visited Susie to say my goodbyes since she'll be heading straight home upon her release. I made sure to leave before everyone else arrived. But now they're back, and I'm in no mood to socialize. Unfortunately, there's a knock at the door, and I have no choice but to let whoever it is in.

"Come in," I say.

"It's me," Maria says as she enters. "We're getting ready to head out, I just need to grab my luggage."

One Christmas With You

I don't say anything in reply. Instead, I continue scrolling through my phone, finalizing my bookings for my upcoming trip and narrowing down the places I want to visit.

"Are you still leaving?" Maria asks.

I look up from my phone and notice her staring at me.

"Why wouldn't I be?" I reply.

"Susie filled us in on what happened," Maria says, her voice low.

"Of course she did."

I put my phone in my pocket and put my hands on the back of my head.

"Listen I don't know Eloise—"

"Let me stop you right there."

I stand. The sound of her name has me on edge.

"Trevor, we've known each other for a long time. This isn't you."

"I don't want to discuss Eloise with you, or with anyone for that matter."

She lets go of her luggage and moves closer to me.

"I know you don't. I know you're hurt."

She waits for confirmation, but all I can do is look at her. She knows me well enough to know that honesty is my one requirement in all my relationships.

She nods, as if my face was saying it all.

"You are the most forgiving person I've ever

known. She made a mistake. You should try to get past it. Fight for her."

She grabs her luggage and starts toward the door but stops short of stepping outside.

"I should've fought for you when you told me you loved me. I was scared. I made a mistake."

I'm not sure what she wants from me. I don't react because there's nothing to react to. She's in my past and I'm not there anymore. I raise an eyebrow as if to say, is there anything else?

"Fight for her before it's too late. Trust me, being on the other side of "it's too late" hurts more," she says before leaving.

As she exits, I realize that her departure means Chase is leaving as well. I feel a pang of sadness because I don't know when I'll see him again. Maybe I'll come back for his wedding, but who knows when that will be.

***

I was ready to put this entire Christmas behind me, including Eloise. All I wanted was to be as far away from the cabin and any reminders of her as possible. I took two photos: one while boarding the plane, and the other when my connecting flight was cancelled indefinitely due to a severe blizzard. When the announcement came through, I couldn't help but laugh at the irony of it all. Escaping things that now reminded me of Eloise wasn't going to be easy after all.

Waiting it out seemed like the only option. Once again, I found myself stuck in an airport, and every step I took led me down memory lane.

As I sat in the waiting area, planning my next move, I contemplated cancelling the entire trip. But then what? I had sold my apartment, my bike, and even my business, for God's sake. I was glad to be alone in the waiting area as I let out an exhausted breath that was louder than I had intended it to be.

I find myself bouncing my leg nervously, like Chase, but it's not helping to calm my racing thoughts. So, I lean forward, placing my elbows on my knees in hopes of stilling the movement. The endless swirl of conversations I've had over the course of this week is making me crazy.

I don't like not knowing my next move or questioning the decisions I've already made. These conversations are penetrating my brain, planting seeds of doubt that are spreading like poison. While I can overcome the doubts that are just starting to sprout, it's the ones that have already taken root that I fear will be much harder to destroy.

Finally, I realized that I was running. I was running from my dad and the life he wanted for me, but now it's no longer necessary. All I ever wanted was his acceptance of my lifestyle and choices. And now that I have it, it feels good, even though it's hard to admit.

Maria was right to turn me down all those years ago. I didn't love her the right way, it was just a knee-jerk reaction after coming out of my trauma. It took me a long time to realize this. Now, I know what love truly is, and it wasn't what I felt for her.

Most importantly, I love Eloise. This realization is difficult to accept, but it's the truth that I can no longer ignore.

In a sudden moment of clarity, it dawns on me that I've wasted enough time at the airport. I quickly grab my bag and head straight to the car rental counter. As I'm making my way there, I dial Susie's number.

CHAPTER 42

Eloise

Work offers the distraction that my apartment couldn't provide. I'm missing Susie like crazy and wish I could have seen the expression on her face when she found out I finally ended things with Chris. Even if she was furious with me, I bet that news still made her smile. I've been working for eight hours straight and have four more hours to go. With any luck, I'll be so exhausted when I get home that sleep will come easily.

The staff is already taking down all the decorations, eager to move on to the next holiday without taking a single moment to reflect on the one that just passed.

During my lunch break, I grab my phone and navigate to Maple Hallow's social media page. The town is still in the holiday spirit. Seeing this made me long to be back there.

A few desserts were brought in by the staff during my break, and it reminded me of baking with Laura back at the cabin. Maybe I can try to bake something when I get home, but who am I kidding? I probably won't have the energy or the stomach for it.

Susie may be gone, but Chris is still around. I've passed him down the corridor a couple of times today. The first time, he pretended not to see me. The second time, he acted like he was discussing me with some new doctor I'd never met before. But I'm not bothered by either interaction because he's not my problem anymore.

***

It's New Year's Eve, and this last week went just about the same as it always does. Different patients with similar problems, and the same old schedule.

When my shift ends, I barely have enough time to make it home for a quick shower before heading over to my parent's place. I grab a small bite to eat before leaving, knowing there will be no eating once I get there.

As I pull into their long driveway, butterflies

begin to form in my stomach. It's a different feeling pulling up to this magnificent house compared to the cozy cabin. I know a familiar chilly reception is waiting for me inside.

I take a deep breath and try to gather my thoughts before knocking on the door. It's now or never. I try to encourage myself. This isn't the first time I've had to steel myself for what's to come.

"Thought you weren't going to make it," my mom says as she greets me.

"Hello," I reply, trying to keep my tone neutral.

I take off my coat and hang it up while she tells me where we're headed. "Your father is waiting in the study.

I roll my eyes at how pretentious she sounds. "Why do you have to call it a study?" I ask.

"Don't be snappy, Eloise," she warns me.

I follow her, continuing to roll my eyes but my irritation quickly turns to shock when I see Chris sitting there with my dad, smoking a cigar and having a drink.

"What the hell?" I blurt out before I can stop myself.

"Watch your language, Eloise," my dad admonishes.

"What is he doing here?"

"Sit down, Eloise," my dad orders.

I hesitate, wanting to run out of there and away

from these people who have betrayed me. But my dad's tone brooks no argument, and I sit down in the big leather chair next to Chris and opposite my parents.

"We heard there was a misunderstanding," starts Dad.

"A misunderstanding?" I blurt.

"Eloise," says Mom, warning me to stand down.

He continues but at this point, I'm more concerned with my numbed hands.

"Chris is willing to forgive you, as are we. As long as you end things with whoever that man was."

My arms have gone numb, and my chest is on fire.

My dad clears his throat and sets down his glass. "Let's get back to business," he says, looking at me. "Eloise, you need to focus on finishing your residency and start thinking about making your relationship more permanent. This will all be behind you soon enough, am I right?" He turns to Chris, extending his glass in a distant, almost forced, cheers.

I feel like I'm in a dream, everything around me is surreal and disconnected. Is this really happening? Is this my life now? I can feel Chris's eyes on me, but I can't bring myself to look at him. I feel like I've been violated like my trust has been shattered into a million pieces.

Chris lifts his glass in response to my dad, but I'm

barely aware of his presence. The room feels like it's spinning around me, and I feel like I'm falling even though I know I'm sitting in the chair. I grip the armrests tightly, but I can barely feel anything through my numb hands.

It's all too much to bear. I want to scream, to lash out, to demand an explanation, but I can't seem to find my voice. I'm trapped in this nightmare, unable to escape.

As they continue talking, their voices fade away into the background. The only voice I can hear is Trevor's, urging me to quit and reminding me that it's my life to live as I choose. My mind circles back to Susie and what she said. *I'm not lucky. I just know what I want and I'm not afraid to go for it. I wanted a baby. So, I got pregnant. I want to raise my baby. So, I quit my job. I'm not afraid of making decisions because my parents will get mad at me.*

"Eloise! Do you hear us?" My mom's yelling my name but it's not until I'm back in the room and away from my thoughts that I hear exactly how loud she's calling me.

"What's the matter with you?" says my dad.

"I told you. She's just not herself," Chris weighs in.

"Enough." I'm a pot that has boiled over.

"Lower your voice," says my dad.

"No," I say even louder.

I stand to face all three of them. My voice is shaking, my heart is racing, and tears are streaming down my face. All the pent-up anger, frustration, and hurt are pouring out of me like a dam that has burst open. I can feel the weight of their expectations, their judgments, and their disappointment lifting off me as I speak. I'm tired of living my life to please others, of suppressing my own desires and dreams. It's time for me to take control, to make my own choices, and to live the life I want.

"Lower your voice, Eloise," Dad demands.

"No. I will not lower my voice. You will hear me once and for all. And I don't care if you don't like it. Or if you never forgive me because I'm not asking for it, not from you," I say to my parents. "And certainly not from you," I say to Chris.

"Eloise—" interrupts my mom, but I don't let her.

"I'm not finished. I'm tired of doing everything to please everyone but myself. No, I will not get back together with you. I would rather be alone for the rest of my life than spend another minute with you."

Chris is in shock.

"And I will not finish my residency. I don't want to be a doctor. There I said it! And I'm done." I breathe what feels like my first breath of the night. "I'm done!" I say quieter this time.

"You cannot quit. You owe us," says my dad, standing to make his point.

"I owe you nothing. But if you want the house you bought, take it. You owe me far more than that. I want my childhood back. My teenage years back. My life."

He stares at me, stunned by my outburst. I glare at both of them waiting for a response, but they're rendered speechless, and I feel great about it.

"You can take whatever material things you want from me that will make you feel better. I only care about one thing and it's not something you have any control over."

My heart is pounding, and my eyes are stinging with tears as I rush out of the office, grabbing my coat and practically sprinting towards the door. I can hear my name being called, but I don't stop. I don't want to hear anything else they have to say. My mind is spinning with anger and frustration, and I feel like I can't breathe. It's not until I'm sitting in my car, gripping the steering wheel, that I allow myself to finally let out a deep, guttural sob. I don't know how long I'm sitting there before I hear my mom knocking on my window.

"Please, Eloise, open the door."

I can feel the anger and frustration boiling inside me, but I take a deep breath and roll down the window.

"What is it?" I say, my voice is neutral.

"Please step out so we can talk."

"No."

"Please."

She places a gentle hand on my arm, and it makes me pause. It's been years since she's shown me any kind of tenderness.

I open the door get out, and lean against it, waiting for her to speak. There's no warmth in my expression as I regard her silently.

"I'm proud of you," she says, and a wave of shock and emotion floods through me. Her face is consumed with sorrow. I'm so confused by her sudden display of emotion that I can only stay silent, allowing her to continue.

"I should've been there for you. I should've stood up for you. I knew you didn't want this. I've known you since you were a kid. But we wanted you to have a good life. A good career," she says, her face heavy with regret.

"Yeah Mom, you should've," I reply, finally facing her.

"You're right," she concedes, and I can see her considering her next words. I simply wait, needing closure with my mom more than ever.

"I know things haven't been easy with your dad. I've tried my best to support his decisions. He decided early on that because you were bright, you should follow in his footsteps. He wanted you to be different from me," she explains tentatively.

"Different from you? What's that supposed to mean?"

I'm feeling cold, tired, and fed up, but I long for honesty from her, so I give her the time she needs to open up and let me in. It dawns on me that this is how Trevor must have felt.

"When your father and I first met, I was on my own, struggling to make ends meet as a college dropout," she reveals, her voice filled with regret.

"After we started dating, things moved quickly between us. Before I knew it, he had finished his residency, and we married shortly after. He insisted that I return to college, and so I did. Against his wishes, I majored in hospitality. He wanted me to strive for something bigger and better, like law, but I couldn't see that for myself," she continues, her tone growing more emotional.

"Eventually, he grew tired of our arguing, and he stopped bringing it up, but he was never truly happy about it. It was a sore subject for sure. I wanted to work at The Plaza. Plan their events and see them come to life. But I never got to. I used to take you there when you were little, especially around Christmas. Do you remember?" she asks, her voice filled with bittersweet memories.

I nod.

"Why didn't you ever tell me about this?"

"Eloise, he's your father and what happens

between him and I shouldn't affect you."

"Except it has, Mom."

She thinks for a moment before answering.

"I suppose so. But look at you. Look at the wonderful woman we raised. You're a doctor, a well-traveled woman. Things turned out well."

"No Mom. They didn't. I've been unhappy for a very long time. And all because you two were trying to live up to some sort of standard that had nothing to do with what your daughter really wanted or needed."

"I know, you're right. That's why I'm here. I don't want to lose you. I don't care if you're a doctor. I truly just want you to be happy."

She places another gentle hand on my arm.

"What happened at the Plaza?" I ask, my heart thumping violently in my chest. I'm scared of what she might say, but I know it's time to face the truth.

She looks down, taking a deep breath before speaking again. "When I had you, a spark reigned within me. I was reminded of the passion I had for hospitality, and I kept talking to your father about going to work—at the Plaza specifically. But he refused to hear any of it," she confesses.

I sense there's more to the story, and I fear she won't tell me the entire truth. So, I nudge her. "And?" I prompt, needing to know.

"He said it was him or the plaza. I chose the plaza."

My hands are warm now, so I take them out of my coat and fold them across my chest.

"So what happened?"

"He said you would be going with him because the plaza was no place to raise a child."

"What?"

"We left New York City the next day and never looked back."

I feel sick.

"Mom, why didn't you fight?"

"Oh Eloise, you of all people know it's not that simple. Besides, it all worked out. Your dad didn't want me working and so I found a creative outlet. I get to host parties and organize events, and I'm very good at it. I have your dad's full support now."

As I listen to my mom's words, I suddenly realize how adept she is at masking her pain. It's so blatantly obvious now, and I feel a pang of sadness for her. I could point out the fact that she settled, but what would be the point? Whatever she's been telling herself to get through these last thirty years has been enough.

"Well, Mom, I'm glad to learn that I'm most like you. Thanks for sharing this with me," I reply, feeling a sense of closeness to her that I haven't felt in years.

"I love you, Eloise," she says, stretching out her arms and asking for a hug that I've been needing from her for a long time.

"Stay in touch, okay?" she adds.

"I will," I promise, feeling a sense of healing and hope that I never thought was possible.

I wait until she's back inside the house before getting into my car. As I sit behind the wheel, my heart is heavy for both of us. We've lost something that we can never get back: time.

But I'm not going to waste another minute. I'm ready to make a change and take control of my life. I drive straight to the hospital to put in my notice.

CHAPTER 43

Eloise

The drive back home was an indistinct blur, but as I neared my house, the weight of the last couple of hours finally hit me like a ton of bricks. The threat of tears loomed behind my eyes, and I made no effort to hold them back as they cascaded down my face. Each tear that fell represented a beautiful thing I had released on this day. With every drop, the reminder that my life was finally my own grew stronger, and I was free to live it on my terms. Trevor would have been proud of me. But in this moment, all I longed for was to talk to Susie, to pour out my heart and soul to her. Oh, how I wished she were here to share this monumental moment with me.

I let out a sigh of relief as I realized that I was almost home, safe from the impending blizzard that was set to hit tonight on New Year's Eve. I'm half aware of my surroundings, still reeling from today's events, when I see a vehicle in my driveway, and then Susie sitting on my porch swing.

I put the car in the park and turned off the engine before getting out slowly. I'm not quite sure what to make of this unexpected visit, and my heart is beating fast with anxiety. I want to make sure everything's alright with Susie, the baby, and Trevor, but I don't even know where to start. I move quickly toward her.

Standing in front of her, my heart pounding with concern, I gently ask, "Is everything okay?"

With a hint of irritation, Susie responds, "You tell me?" I can sense the anger in her voice, and I don't blame her.

"I know I owe you an explanation. Trevor and I—"

"I don't care about you and Trevor. I thought we were best friends, Eloise?"

"We are," I say, sitting next to her.

"Then why didn't you trust me to tell me about what Chris did to you? Or that you met some amazing guy six months ago?"

As I sit next to Susie, her words ringing in my ears, I feel a sense of regret. My mind is racing as I try to understand why I didn't share anything with her.

"You should've told me that Chris cheated on you

so I could have been there for you. And although I would normally not want my friend and my brother to be a thing, I confess that it would've been different with you. And I don't care that you and Trev had a thing. I only wish it had been more," Susie says, placing her hand on mine.

When she touches my hand, something inside me breaks, and I can no longer hold back my tears. I break down, my body wracked with sobs as I realize how much I have hurt my friend.

I clutch Susie's hand, holding onto her for dear life as the tears pour down my face. I know we can work through this and come out stronger on the other side.

"I'm sorry. I'm so sorry," I cry, hugging her.

"It's okay. It's okay."

She pats my back, and a sense of comfort washes over me. I feel like I can breathe again, and that everything is going to be okay. I pull back from her embrace, feeling a newfound sense of hope, and then I ask the question that's been on my mind since she last called me.

"Did you change…" I don't know why, but I'm afraid to know the answer, so I circle around it, "The baby, did you change her name?"

"Are you insane?" she says, hitting my arm. "Why would I do that?"

"I thought you were angry with me."

"I was. But that's what happens with family. We get mad. Then we get over it. She's still my precious Eloise, and so are you," she says, playfully poking me.

"I have so much to tell you, but let's get inside. It's freezing," I say.

Over the next hour, I poured my heart out to Susie, telling her everything that's been weighing on me lately. I tell her about my parents' and Chris's infidelity, and how I finally took the plunge and resigned.

Susie is surprised to hear that Chris wanted to work things out even after seeing me with Trevor. She is appalled that my parents wanted me to sweep what he did under the rug just to save face. But above all, she's proud of me for taking control of my life and making the decisions that were best for me.

As Susie's words of encouragement sink in, I feel a sense of pride swelling in my chest. For the first time in a long time, I feel like I'm on the right path, and that everything is going to be okay. I smile at Susie, feeling grateful for her unwavering support and love.

I couldn't hold back my curiosity any longer, and I asked her if Trevor had left. When she confirmed that he had, I felt like the ground beneath me gave way. All hope for reconciliation was lost. Up until that moment, I had been holding onto the hope that he would find it in his heart to forgive me and trust me once again. But now, that hope was shattered into a million pieces. Tears streamed down my face as I realized the magnitude of my mistakes. I had lost him, and I knew deep down that I had no one to blame but myself.

CHAPTER 44

Trevor

I've been driving for hours, with the blizzard chasing me all the way back to Georgia. It's not the ideal way to spend New Year's Eve, but I can't think of a better way to start the year off than with Eloise at my side, that is if everything goes well.

The only person who knows that I didn't make it to Europe is Susie. I asked her not to say anything when I called and asked for Eloise's address. I'm now moments away from pulling into her driveway.

I'm nervous as I park my car and step out into the snow. The flakes fall all around me, swirling in the wind, as I make my way up to Eloise's doorstep. I'm not sure what to expect when I see her, and I don't know if it's too late to make things right. My hands are sweaty despite the freezing weather. What if she doesn't want to see me? I knock on the door, my heart pounding in my chest.

It's a gentle knock. But when the seconds drag on, I try again.

"Trevor," she says, surprise dripping from her voice.

"Can I come in?"

"Of course."

She opens the door, welcoming me inside. As I move past her, I notice the oversized T-shirt she's wearing, barely covering her thighs. She has paired it with high Christmas socks and is holding a glass of wine in her hand. It is the best sight I have seen all day.

Her home, while tidy, wasn't as bright and joyful as I expected for the Christmas-loving Eloise I know. In the background, the annual New Year celebration is on, with only ten minutes left until midnight.

I'm no longer nervous. I'm sure of why I'm here and what I want. I'm ready to start telling her, but before I begin, she beats me to it.

"I thought you were in Europe?" she asks.

"My flight got cancelled."

She smiles, catching the irony.

"Want to sit?" she offers, gesturing to the couch.

"No."

"Okay. Wine?" she asks, pointing to the almost empty wine glass in her hand.

I shake my head.

She watches me anxiously.

"What then," she asks.

"I want you, Eloise," I finally confess.

Her lips turn into a sweet, but disbelieving smile. And it's confirmation that I'm not too late.

"You see, I've been on this journey for years now. The journey of just one. I thought you were part of that journey. Just one night. Just one Christmas. 'I'll be fine,' I kept telling myself. But as it turns out, the power of one didn't work out so well this time. One kiss from you only made me want more. One night with you made me need more. And one Christmas with you sure as hell wasn't enough," I confess.

It had been five days since I last touched or held her, and I don't know how I managed to hold out for so long. But I couldn't hold back any longer. I move closer to her, taking her face in my hands, and kiss her gently but briefly, as I need to see her face. Her eyes are filled with tears until she releases them. The emotion in the air was palpable.

"I love you," I say.

In the background, I was aware of the countdown that had begun: five, four, three, two, one. Happy New Year! The crowd cheered. But all I could focus on was Eloise's lips, as I kissed her at the start of the

One Christmas With You

new year and my new life.

Epilogue

Eloise

Six months later

The transition from doctor to business owner has been challenging, to say the least. But with Trevor's unwavering support, I have managed to navigate the uncharted waters of entrepreneurship, focusing solely on what I love most – baking.

As I sit in the back office of my new bakery, with my eyes fixed on the spreadsheet in front of me, I have a sense of pride and satisfaction. I've crossed all the T's and dotted all the I's, and everything is set for my grand opening.

For the first time in a long time, I feel like I'm

truly living. I'm doing what I love, and I'm finally able to share my passion with the world. It's a dream come true, and I'm emotional as I take in the significance of the moment.

As I take a deep breath and close my eyes, I know that the journey ahead won't be easy. But with every challenge that comes my way, I'll remind myself of this moment – the moment when I realized that I'm living the life I've always wanted and that nothing can bring me down.

When it came to finding the perfect location for my bakery, I didn't have to look very far. I knew exactly where I wanted to set up shop – a place that celebrated Christmas and all the holidays with the same enthusiasm and love that I did.

Maple Hollow wasn't just about Christmas. Every single holiday and special event mattered here, and I was confident that my bakery would fit right in.

I moved out of the house and moved in with Trevor. Moving in together was a bold step for us both. But we found a cozy cabin near the mountains, closer to Maple Hollow.

Today is the day of my bakery's grand opening, and I am feeling a mixture of excitement and nerves that I can't seem to shake. Over the past few months, I have received a lot of help from my new and old friends. Laura has been instrumental in helping me create the perfect menu, while Susie has acted as my trusty taste tester. Since Ava and Chase live close by, Ava helped me design an inviting and charming bakery that I am proud of.

Of course, I could not have done this without Trevor. He has been my rock and source of unwavering support throughout this entire process. Even while he was busy opening a new gym, he still made time to help me out whenever he could. His business skills made it possible for us to open the bakery quickly, and I am so grateful for all that he has done.

I stand to head out, but before I do, I take a glance in the mirror—something that Ava forced me to include. She said a mirror was a must. As I look at my reflection, it feels like I'm staring at someone else, living someone else's life. Why did it take me so long to become this person?

I've asked myself this question a thousand times since New Year's Eve. The easy answer would be to place all the blame on my parents, but that would be a lie. The truth is that I hold some blame too. If only I had spoken up sooner, things would have been different for me.

For years, I believed that my voice didn't matter, and so I remained silent. I thought that expressing myself would be pointless because it wouldn't make a difference. But I was wrong. It only took one moment of pure honesty to change my life, just one moment.

I often wonder what my life could have been like if I'd had the courage to speak up years ago.

Although my relationship with my parents is not exactly perfect, we are starting anew with much integrity. I am building a strong foundation now so that it can withstand any weather, just like my winning snowman. However, there are boundaries, which means they have zero say in my life, including when I call, when I visit, and who I date. They've met Trevor, and while my mom was courteous, my dad was his usual self. He barely spoke and ultimately excused himself, claiming that work was calling. Although I would have loved his approval, I no longer need it.

I make my way to the front of the store, where Susie is seated at one of the small round tables, busy adding napkins to the dispenser. She's been by my side all morning, helping me wipe counters, label jars, and offering moral support.

Dave should be here any minute with the baby, along with the rest of the family. I grab a seat next to her and peek outside. There is already a crowd waiting.

"How are you doing?" she says, finishing up.

She doesn't wait for me to answer before she checks in again.

"Are you ready?" she says, looking around the shop.

It takes me a minute before I answer because I haven't really taken the time to think it through. I've been full of adrenaline, trying to get here.

As I look around the bakery, I am enchanted by the sight of charming cabinetry and glass displays showcasing an array of pastel cupcakes, cakes, and other sweet delights. The decor is everything I had imagined it to be, elegant and inviting, with a touch of whimsy.

The interior is warm and cozy, with soft lighting and a welcoming atmosphere that invites you to stay a while. The shelves are lined with beautifully crafted confections, each one more tempting than the last. From delicate cupcakes adorned with swirls of buttercream frosting to towering layer cakes dripping with chocolate ganache, there is something for every sweet tooth here.

And the exterior is just as lovely, with a classic design that blends elements of Christmas with a celebration of all holidays. The storefront is adorned with twinkling lights, and a welcome sign crafted by Grandpa Carl beckons visitors inside.

"I am," I finally say.

Once I do, I hear another voice from the back of the shop.

"How's my girl doing?" says Trevor, flashing me a grin that lights up the whole room.

He makes a beeline towards me and kisses me on

my lips. I feel more ready than ever.

"I'm great. I'm ready to open the doors."

"Let's do this. But one second," he says, running back inside the office.

He comes back with his camera.

"Stand right there," he points to a part of the wall where the shop's name is displayed; One Sweet Bite.

I do as he says, and he snaps a few photos.

"Now you're ready." He says with a wink, stepping aside.

With a grateful nod, I look at both of them, feeling an immense sense of appreciation for their presence in my life. There is no one else I'd rather share my journey with than them.

I make my way to the door, feeling a mix of excitement and nervousness as I flip the sign from "closed" to "open." As I step outside, I greet the crowd of people eagerly waiting, and a surge of emotion wells up inside me.

With a smile on my face and a welcoming gesture, I invite everyone inside. "Please come in."

As the room fills with chatter and laughter, I'm keenly aware that I am exactly where I'm supposed to be.

THE END!

THANK YOU!

Thanks a ton for reading my novel! It's pretty awesome to think about someone diving into the world I've created.

I poured my heart and soul into this story, hoping it would bring a smile to your face or maybe even keep you up past your bedtime turning pages.

If you end up loving it as much as I do, would you mind spreading the word on Amazon? A quick review would totally make my day and help other readers discover the magic within these pages.

Thanks a million for being part of this adventure with me. Here's to many more stories to come!

Review Here:
https://amzn.to/3PLl6BN

ABOUT THE AUTHOR

I'm a small-town romance writer who's always dreamed of living in the quaint, charming settings that fill my books. Now, I'm living that dream in a small town that inspires every page I write. I love sharing snippets of my life and my writing journey on social media, inviting you to experience the romance and charm of small-town life with me. Join me for stories that come straight from the heart of my own little slice of heaven.

Falling For You
Between Us
Choose Us

Visit Mari Suggs at:

www.marisuggs.com
YouTube: YouTube.com/marisuggs
TikTok: TikTok.com/@authormarisuggs
Instagram: Instagram.com/marisuggs

www.ingramcontent.com/pod-product-compliance
Lightning Source LLC
LaVergne TN
LVHW031609060526
838201LV00065B/4790